Carl Weber's Kingpins:

Chicago

Carl Weber's Kingpins:
Chicago

Silk Smooth

URBAN BOOKS

www.urbanbooks.net

Urban Books, LLC
97 N18th Street
Wyandanch, NY 11798

ISBN 13: 978-1-62286-727-1
ISBN 10: 1-62286-727-0

First Trade Paperback Printing August 2016
Printed in the United States of America

10 9 8 7 6 5 4 3 2

Distributed by Kensington Publishing Corp.
Submit Orders to:
Customer Service
400 Hahn Road
Westminster, MD 21157-4627
Phone: 1-800-733-3000
Fax: 1-800-659-2436

BONES

The streets of Chicago weren't shit to play with. Been running those muthafuckas since I was ten years old. Years later, I was still trying to run them or trying to run from them. Many niggas had a kill-or-be-killed mentality, but the only thing I was trying to do, at the present time, was save myself from becoming a statistic. In order to do that, I had to refocus and do whatever to stay on a straight and narrow path. It damn sure wasn't easy, but day by day, I was making progress.

The problem was knowing too many people. I basically knew every single individual on my block, and then some. So when niggas who weren't from around here showed up, I could sniff them out a mile away. Either they were here to do some gangbanging shit, or a plan was put in motion for somebody in the hood to die. There were plenty of times when weak niggas turned to me to handle their beefs. I didn't mind. My reputation was stellar. My word, bond. If I told a person what I was gon' do, ten times out of ten, it got done.

That was then, the past. Today was a new day, and I excluded myself from much of the madness that was being reported on the news, every single day. It was sad to see sometimes, but it all boiled down to one simple thing—choices. Within the last year, I'd made mine. I wanted to live. Live life to the fullest, at least until I was 110 years old. To me, that was a possibility. And as far as I knew, I didn't have no beefs with any of the niggas around here. My boys, Theo and Nate, I wasn't so sure. They were involved in all kinds of illegal shit, and making the almighty dollar by any means necessary was their priority. I had no problem with the route they'd chosen, and it didn't bother me one bit because I was known as being boss . . . a leader, not a follower. And when all was mulled over and done, those two would still be my niggas.

We all had been down with each other since grade school. Our family situations were about the same—absentee fathers, mothers dead, on drugs, or in prison. I kicked back with my grandmother, Theo resided with his aunt, Lala, and Nate was here and there. Wherever he could lay his head, that was home for him.

Many times, Nate shacked up at my grandmother's house or with Theo and his aunt. Then he hooked up with a chick named Alexis. When she got pregnant and had his child, the two of them got a place on Section 8. I was surprised by how quickly Nate had pulled back on his womanizing ways. He was known for being out there with a whole lot of bitches, but I was happy for him. That was . . . until I found out how much he got a thrill out of kicking Alexis's ass. He had always been the abusive type. Theo and I feared that Nate would kill Alexis one day . . . only because Nate had a temper that would flare up at the drop of a dime.

Years ago, it wasn't Nate's temper that got us expelled from high school. It was mine. I/we beat the fuck out of two teachers who snitched on us. As the beatings took place in an alley, I delivered my "specialty" and cracked plenty of bones. I got high off doing that shit; they didn't call me Bones for nothing. The snaps, pops . . . cracks gave me a rush and left me with the feeling of pure satisfaction. It was my revenge for those who somehow or someway made me suffer, like those fake-ass teachers did. We left school in handcuffs that day, and after spending several months in juvie, education was a wrap.

Without a diploma, I opted for fucked-up jobs at McDonald's, Burger King . . . even a sales job at the mall. That's where I worked now, but I hated smiling in muthafuckas' faces, pretending that I was happy to be there making chump change. Theo and Nate laughed at my ass for working as a sales representative, but I promised my grandmother that I would do better. After all she'd done for me, I didn't want to disappoint her. I didn't want her to think that her efforts had been wasted, but I'd be the first to admit that the way my job situation had been going, change was coming.

"Bones!" my flamboyant supervisor hissed, then snapped his fingers. "This customer needs some help. Pleeease put that down and hurry yourself over here. I don't know where Sally is, but you need to step up when she's somewhere stuffing her fat little ass with cake."

This dude was a trip. Whoever hired him needed to be fired. I had been hanging some new leather jackets on a rack in the men's section and hadn't seen the ugly bitch standing nearby with a twisted face. I also didn't appreciate my supervisor's tone, but sometimes shit like this had to be ignored. I put the jackets down and sluggishly walked up to the customer.

"What do you need?" I said.

My supervisor rolled his eyes and stomped away like a little bitch. "A smile never hurt anybody," he said underneath his breath. "I don't know what his problem is."

I wanted to fire back at him, but I had grown skillful at ignoring people.

With an attitude, the chick pointed to a yellow shirt that her five-two frame was unable to reach. At six feet tall, it was no problem for me.

"Reach up there to get that for me," she said. "I need it in a small, if you have it."

A small? Seriously? I thought. More like a triple X. She wasn't about to squeeze all of that into a small, but maybe she was looking at the shirt for someone else.

I pulled down the shirt and gave it to her. She held it in front of her, and then asked where the dressing rooms were.

"The lady's dressing room is in the far back to the left. Men's room to the right."

She winced and cut her eyes at me. "For a man who is so darn fine and who smells very delicious, you're not too bright, are you? I didn't ask where the men's dressing room was. I said girls. Do I look like a man to you?"

She really didn't want me to answer her. Hell fucking yeah, she did. I bit down on my tongue so I didn't have to share my inner thoughts with this overweight, stank-breath bitch whose compliments didn't move me in no way. All I did was point in the direction of the fitting room, and then I walked away. I was one to believe . . . treat others as they treat you. She didn't encourage me to represent my true professionalism. Seconds later, my supervisor approached me.

"Are you *special*, Bones? I saw the way you treated that customer. I'm warning you about this attitude problem of yours. It needs to cease or else."

I rubbed the fine hair on my chin while staring at my supervisor without a blink. He had no idea who he was fucking with. Pushing my buttons was a huge mistake. I cocked my neck to the side, then cleared my throat. "I'ma finish hanging up these jackets. Then I'm taking my break."

Doing the norm, he rolled his eyes, threw his hands in the air, then stomped away. I hurried to hang the rest of the jackets, and then clocked out so I could go to the food court to get some grub. On my way out, I accidentally bumped into a fine-ass black chick that was with two other people.

"Sorry about that," I said, picking up the bag she dropped and gave it back to her.

The smile on her face got wide. Her eyes traveled from my flowing waves to the leather shoes on my feet.

"No problem at all. I wasn't paying attention to where I was going, and I hope that I didn't hurt your shoulder when I bumped it."

She reached out to touch my muscular shoulder that formed an impression in the ocean-blue, crisp shirt I rocked. It was tucked neatly into my black jeans, and a leather belt was at my waistline, making me look neat. I moved her hand from my shoulder and told her everything was fine.

"Yes, you are. And rather sexy too. I know you must have a million-and-one girlfriends."

I wasn't trying to have this conversation, especially with someone who I didn't know. From the look in my eyes, she could tell it was time to move on.

"Have a nice day," she said, still smiling. "And don't hurt nobody with those looks."

I walked off, revisiting some of my past relationships in my head. I had a difficult time expressing my feelings, and none of my relationships lasted for long. Whenever I felt myself getting too close, I shut the shit down. Why? Because most females were trouble. Like niggas, they plotted and schemed too. They lied. Cheated. Manipulated. Claimed to love when they didn't, and then pretended to be victims. Fuck that. The only time I wanted to deal was when I had an urge to quietly slip in, then get the fuck out.

After paying for my food, I sat at the table eating chicken and rice, thinking about the last chick I directed my dick into. She was a stripper. Met her while we were out celebrating Theo's birthday. Fucked her in one of the stalls. She got hers. I got mine. I left. That was about two . . . three months ago. Pussy was fire, but I couldn't even tell you her name. Nate was the one who revealed to me that her name was Red. She made it too easy for me and had proven one fact—pussy came a dime a dozen. How in the hell was any nigga supposed to be faithful? I didn't believe that anyone could be, especially since being unfaithful to her so-called boyfriend, pimp, or whoever the fuck he was, had cost my mother her life. I watched in horror as she paid the price for cheating on a fool who was cheating on her.

I was awakened from my sleep that night. Mama and her boyfriend, Stan, were arguing. She had been out all night long, and like always, she strutted through the door with her hair disheveled and wrinkles throughout her clothes. Her makeup was smeared, and the look of "I just got fucked well" was written all over her. She took slow steps back into a corner, while Stan moved forward, gritting his stained teeth. His fists were tightened. Chest heaved in and out and sweat ran over the thick wrinkles lining his forehead.

"I can smell that foul pussy all the way over here. The second you came through the door, I could tell that you'd been somewhere fucking that nigga again! Don't you lie to me, woman! The smell of his dick is still on yo' breath!"

Mama crouched down in the corner and kept on with her lies. Her hands trembled as she held them together, hoping and praying that Stan would fall back and chill.

"Stan, baby, please. God knows I wouldn't cheat on you. I was with Jasmine. We had a few drinks, and then . . . then we drove to her mother's crib to drop off some groceries. On the way back, she had car trouble. We were stuck for a long while. Didn't nobody stop to help us."

I peered through the brown wooden rails on the steps, looking at Mama and knowing that she had fucked her-

self. Jasmine had already been here earlier. Stan waxed that ass, gave her some paper, and then she left. They'd been fucking behind Mama's back for years. I wasn't sure if she'd known about it, but young boy or not, I paid attention to what was transpiring around me.

"Bitch, stop lying!" Stan yelled and staggered closer. He was drunk as hell. Spit flew from his mouth as he called Mama all kinds of trifling bitches and hoes. "I want the truth! I want to know where the fuck you were at! I want you to call that nigga and tell him that you're done!"

Mama wiped his spit from her face. She pressed her knees against her chest and continued to shiver in the tight corner. "Stan, you're delusional. I . . . I promise you that I ain't been with—"

Stan silenced her lies with a swift kick to her face, provided by the bottom of his foot. Her head knocked against the wall so hard that it caused a dent. While holding the back of her head, she squirmed against the wall, attempting to stand. That was when he snatched her up by the back of her hair and slung her toward the kitchen. She skidded across the dirty tile floor, appearing weak and dazed. Stan stood over her, darting his finger at her face.

"Are you ready to tell me where you've been?" He punted her in the stomach, and as she curled herself into a fetal position, she screeched and pleaded for him to stop.

I inched my way down a few more steps, just so I could see more of what was happening. My heart ached for Mama. The last time I intervened, she yelled at me. Told me to keep my black ass out of grown folks' business. I wasn't sure if I should've done something or not. Stan was way bigger than I was, but I was strong for my age. I wasn't sure where my strength had come from, but I'd gotten in trouble at school often for wrestling with the other kids and causing major injuries when they upset me. Mama never did much about me getting in trouble; therefore, I had gotten out of control. She was too busy prostituting herself and selling dope. I'd heard her tell one of her friends one day that she hated I was born. She hated me and wished she had aborted me. In her view, my grandmother could do a better job raising me than she could. She was right, and it wasn't that I hated her for saying such cruel things, but that shit affected me. It affected our relationship. We didn't have one. My love for her just wasn't there, but I still needed her. I felt bad about how Stan was treating her. Watching him do her that way brought hella tears to my eyes.

"O . . . okay," Mama yelled out as she scrambled to get away from him. He kicked her in the ass this time, and she fell flat on the floor. "I . . . I'll tell you, but pleeeease stoooop this!"

He stood over her looking like a madman. More sweat ran from his forehead, and his eyes were real wide. He wiped across his thick, ashy lips, waiting for Mama's confession.

"I was with Carl." She dropped her head in shame. "I've been spending time with Carl because I knew you'd been fucking that bitch Jasmine!"

There was no secret that Stan didn't like Carl. Mama could screw any other nigga that Stan wanted her to. Not Carl. He was Stan's enemy. The truth in no way set Mama free. What it did was cause him to go crazy. The cold, sinister look trapped in his eyes alerted me that something heavy was about to go down. He grabbed Mama's long hair and wrapped it around his hand. While dragging her across the floor, her legs flopped like fishes as she kicked and screamed for him to release her.

"You said the truth would set me free!" Mama cried out. *"Why won't you just let me be and leave me the hell alone!"*

Stan yanked open a drawer and pulled out a long, shiny knife with a sharp-ass blade. I rushed into the kitchen, and while standing in nothing but my dingy underwear, I pleaded with Stan too.

"Don't hurt my mama." I smacked tears away from my face. Didn't want him to think I was soft, and crying was for punks. *"Please, please, don't kill my mama. She all I got."*

Stan had a smirk on his face while gazing at me. Then the nigga had the nerve to laugh. The direction of my eyes moved to Mama. I was upset with her for bringing this coldhearted animal in our house, and how in the fuck could she put a nigga like him before me? I wanted to ask, but the sad look in her eyes, as she looked at me, said she was sorry. She knew better, but it was too late.

"Go, baby," she said to me. *"Go to your grandmother's house. Get out of here before he hurt you too. He will hurt you, and I don't want you to leave here like this."*

I refused to leave her. Shook my head from side to side, indicating no. *"No, Mama, I . . . I can't leave you."* Snot dripped from my nose as I threatened Stan, hoping to put some fear in him. *"Put the knife down or else I'ma call the police. You gon' go to jail, and those niggas in there gon' beat you up!"*

Stan laughed, then raised the knife over his head. *"Call the police and tell them what? That yo' Mama is a ho, and I did this to her?"*

He dropped his hand and plunged the knife right into the center of Mama's chest. She and I gasped at the same time. My breathing stopped. Face twisted and stomach tightened in a knot. Mama's sad facial expression tore at my heart and soul. Salty tears streamed down my *face as I saw her eyes pleading for me to do something. She even reached out her trembling hand for me to hold it. I rushed forward, and that was when Stan had his way. He yanked the knife out of her chest and jabbed it in—again and again. At least fifteen to twenty more times. Her blood sprayed my body and soaked every inch of the clothing she had on. Her head was tilted, and Stan dropped her to the floor as if she wasn't shit.*

"Now," he said, swiping his hands together, "you can call the police on me."

I tried to speak but couldn't say one word. Thought I was dreaming, but unfortunately, this was my reality. I blinked away my tears and saw a blurred vision of Mama lying dead on the floor in a pool of thick blood. I lost it. Ran up to Stan, and he lifted his hand high again.

"Think before you act, li'l nigga," he said. "I ain't got no beef with you, but if you want to die today, that's fine with me."

I didn't care about dying. So fucking be it. Stan would do me a favor by killing me. I charged him, and in an instant, I felt the knife slice me above the brow. On my chin. My hand and somewhere on my back. In the midst of me trying to overpower him, I heard gunfire. Several bullets whistled through the air and one of them tore into Stan's forehead. His body wobbled, then dropped on top of mine, damn near crushing me as we both hit the floor. All I remembered after that was seeing a gang of police officers surrounding us. The next day, I woke up in the hospital with my grandmother praying by my side.

My break was over too soon. After I cleared my thoughts of what had happened that day, I chalked up my feelings and strolled with confidence back to work.

"He got that Curtis Jackson, 50 Cent swag," one chick proclaimed as I walked smoothly by her and a friend.

I had heard the same comment before, but the way I saw it, *I* was an original. I tossed my head back and kept it moving. The second I walked through the door, my supervisor was at it again.

"You only have one minute left. By the time you go to the back and clock in, you'll be considered late. This is totally ridiculous. I'm not going to keep babysitting you. Don't bother to clock back in. I'll be sure to have your check mailed to you by the end of the week."

I lifted my hand, causing his frail ass to jump back in fear. All I did was scratch my head, pretending as if I was the idiot he proclaimed me to be. "So, what you're saying is I'm fired, right?"

He confirmed. "Yes. F-I-R-E-D, fired!"

I glanced at several people standing around, watching the whole scene. Mr. Drama Queen had put on quite a show. But there was a time and place for everything. Now wasn't the time, so I responded with a shrug.

"It's all good," I said. "Just make sure I get my check."

Without responding, he walked off. I went to the back to swoop up my belongings, then left. Every eye was still on me. Was I embarrassed? Hell yeah, I was. One lady stopped me as I headed for the main exit doors.

"That was totally uncalled for back there," she said. "I don't appreciate the way he spoke to you. If I were you, I would call his boss."

"It's not worth it to me," I said to the concerned woman. "Muthafuckas like that always get what's coming to them."

She nodded. "You got that shit right. God bless you. I hope you find another job."

I was sure that somewhere down the road I would. I thanked the woman and parted ways with her as she went to her car and I went to mine. I chilled inside for a while, thinking. Unemployed, again. Dissed, again.

Disrespected, no doubt. Two steps up, five back. That's what my boy Nate always said. I couldn't resist calling to tell him just how right he was. I knew that he and Theo would laugh and make fun of me for getting fired, and you best believe, when I hit Nate with the breaking news, he cracked up.

"Man, I told you about dealing with those two-bit-ass jobs. You need to come play where the real players play. I don't know, nor do I understand, what is holding you back."

"You already know what's up. I can't be taking no risks like y'all do. The last thing my ass want to do is spend my life in jail. I'd rather put up with the bullshit out here, than deal with the bullshit in there."

"I feel you, bro, but sometimes, taking risks pays off. And the last time I checked, ain't nothing wrong with doing what you must to stay afloat and keep a li'l change in yo' pockets."

We'd had this debate plenty of times before. I just wasn't down with selling drugs, robbing folks, gambling, or pimping hoes. Making money by any means necessary wasn't my motto, but at the rate I had been going with these jobs, I had to rethink some shit.

"We'll talk about my situation later. Meanwhile, what did ol' girl cook today? I know she done hooked you up."

"Not yet, but a late dinner is being prepared. I got home earlier and there wasn't nothing on the table. Told that bitch to get off Facebook and make some music with pots and pans. She working on something now. Stop by, if you want to."

"Most definitely. Give me about an hour and I'll be there."

After I ended my call with Nate, I removed my dress shirt and relaxed the seat back. I still sported my white, V-neck T-shirt that displayed an array of tats on both arms. My entire back was covered with BONES tattooed in script across it. I still wanted more on my chest, but that shit was costly. Money was an issue.

I removed a joint from my pocket. Started to get high and filled the car with a cloud of smoke as I released some of it into the air. It had gotten dark outside, but I kept watching the exit door. When I spotted my supervisor come outside, I positioned my seat up straight. I massaged my strong hands together while eyeing my target, as well as several cameras that I assumed wouldn't get a clear picture of me or my license plates, because it was too dark. I was thankful for broken parking lot lights that made it easier for criminals to shake and move. Even easier for me, as I saw my supervisor looking down, searching for his keys. By the time he looked up, he bumped right into my hard chest.

"Excuse me—"

My dark eyes narrowed. His mouth clamped tight and fear washed over him. That pleased me, more than ever. I reached up and gripped his red neck. Squeezed so tight that he could barely breathe. He scratched at my hands as I shoved him against his car and lifted him from the ground. His feet dangled. Pleading, watery eyes begged for me to let him go.

"D-E-A-D, dead. That's what you will be, if you keep disrespecting muthafuckas, and if you open yo' mouth about this problem you now have to anyone, I know where you live, *and* I know where you work. Consider this payback for all of yo' bullshit and referring to me as, 'the stupid nigger over there who don't do shit.' FYI, here's what I can do."

Tears seeped from the corners of his eyes, and his whole face turned beet red. He thought he was in the clear when I released my grip, and when he doubled over to cough and soothe his neck with his hands, I reached for his arm, pulling it behind his back.

"Pluu . . . please," he said between coughs and spit foaming from his mouth. "I . . . I'm sorry."

So was I. Sorry that I hadn't done this sooner. I used my overpowering strength to twist his arm and stretch it, tight, eventually breaking it in two places. The loud snaps caused him to yelp in excruciating pain and drop to his knees.

"Ahhhhhhhhhhh, ahhhhhh, ahhhhh," he hollered out while holding his limp arm that required immediate attention. His screams had awakened the dead, so I rushed to my car and sped off. I thought about running that muthafucka over, but seeing him in much pain satisfied me enough. Enough to make me wash the serious look off my face for only a few seconds, and smile.

BONES

Theo, Nate, and I sat at the table smoking blunts, talking shit, and drinking a mixture of alcohols. Alexis was in the kitchen putting the finishing touches on the food. Their daughter, Brianna, was in her bedroom playing video games with her cousin Jo. YG's "Who Do You Love?" thumped in the background, and a comedy show was in and out on the TV.

Nate made a comment about Theo's whack haircut that made him look even more like a nerd. He patted the top part of his tiny fro, then rubbed his shaved sides. "Stop hating, nigga. It's not a good look for you. I'ma ignore you, though, and get back to Mr. Bones. I thought you were done breaking bones and necks. That fool must've really pissed you the fuck off!"

I shrugged from across the table, pretending as if it was nothing. "As they say . . . You get in return what you put out. He deserved it."

Nate twirled his brown liquids around in a glass. He stood and washed the liquids down his throat, then cleared it. "He lucky you didn't kill him. I would have done so, and we already know that Bones is weak."

I jumped up from my chair and gave Nate a playful pound to his chest. He staggered backward while smiling. I always thought of Ludacris when I saw Nate, and if he'd had Luda's paper, we'd all be good. I tried to punch him again, but this time he dodged my punch.

"Back the fuck up!" he laughed. "I don't want you breakin' shit over here. I was just playing about the weak thing so don't go scheming on beating me down later."

I returned to my seat, then put the bottle of alcohol up to my lips. "That's what I thought. Rethink that shit, take two aspirin, and holla at me in the morning."

Nate laughed again. Pulled up his sagging gray sweats and slid into his Nike sandals. "What in the hell is taking this slow bitch so long?" he whispered. "Did she fall asleep?"

Looking dope as always with her straight, long hair parted through the middle and resting on her breasts, Alexis came through the swinging door with two plates in her hand. "No, the slow bitch didn't."

One plate was piled high with crispy chicken, the other with mac & cheese. The aroma breezed through the air as she passed by me.

"Smelling good," I said, eyeing the food as she put it on the table.

"I know, baby. I do smell good, don't I?" She pursed her lips, shot Nate a dirty look, and then sashayed back into the kitchen.

"Baby?" Nate said. "Who in the fuck is she referring to as her baby?"

"Who cares?" Theo said, snatching up a piece of chicken. "I'm hungry, and this sholl look good to me."

I was starving too, but I wanted to wait until Nate and the kids got their food. He still seemed a little irritated, though, and he paced while holding his manhood.

"Nigga, don't trip," I said. "She didn't mean nothing by that shit. You know she was just playing."

For a minute, I thought he was playing too, but as soon as Alexis came through the door with buttered rolls, he approached her with wide eyes.

"What's up with the baby thing, li'l mama? Since when do you think it's okay to refer to one of my boys as your baby?"

Alexis waved him off. She put the buttered rolls on the table and pulled back a chair to take a seat. Catching everyone off guard, Nate raised his fist and slammed it at the side of her face. The blow was so hard that it sent her flying out of the chair and on the floor. I jumped from my seat, and so did Theo. He didn't like this kind of shit—there was no secret; I didn't either. We had seen it play out time and time again, between Nate and his other bitches. This, however, was the first time I witnessed him get at Alexis like that, even though I knew he had done it before. She shielded her face with her hands and started to weep.

"Damn, man," Theo said with disgust washed across his face. "Why you tripping? You ain't have to do that."

Nate was on some shit that I couldn't comprehend. "That bitch don't disrespect me, then blow me off. Answer me when I ask you a question, dammit!"

I tried to help Alexis off the floor, but she pushed me away. That's when I turned to Nate, already knowing that heat would swing my way for taking up for her. My voice was calm because I didn't want to argue with him. These days, anything would set him off.

"You need to chill with that shit, man. It wasn't even that serious, and I have to ask what in the hell is wrong with you?"

He sucked his teeth, then dropped back in the chair. "I'm glad you asked, 'cause I'm about to give you an earful. What's wrong with me is I got a bitch that don't do nothing all damn day but talk to her friends, laugh at vine videos, and lollygag on Facebook. I need somebody to help me pay the goddamn bills around here, but this bitch sit on her ass all day doing nothing but looking pretty. Even her pussy ain't about nothing anymore. Ask that ho when the last time she's offered me some of that without me having to take it. I take too many risks and work too hard out there in them streets to be dissed in my own home. If she could, at least, get a job at Hooters or something, then maybe I can accept some shit. Until then, I demand my fucking respect, *and* I need a bitch in my life who is motivated!"

Alexis lifted her head. A red, swollen mark had formed on her light skin, right next to her eye. She mean mugged Nate and finally spoke up.

"You ain't shit, Nate. I swear you ain't shit! The rent here is fifty damn dollars a month, and if you think you should be praised for paying that, sorry. It ain't gon' happen! If yo' boys want an earful, here it is. I get assistance for the electric bill, Brianna goes to school for free, and the water and trash bills total less than twenty bucks a month. Food is paid for by the government, and most of the clothes we wear are sold to us by shoplifters who I pay less than half price! You can beat my ass all you want to, but I have to appreciate what a nigga does for me, in order for me to up this pussy. You are not deserving, and I wish—God, I wish like hell—that you would get the fuck out of *my* house!"

A look of embarrassment came across Nate's face. He charged toward Alexis, but Theo and I held him back. Well, truthfully, I did. Theo was too skinny, and he was, what I considered, the weakest link of us all.

"Go," I said to Nate, shoving him backward. "Go somewhere and cool off. We'll catch up later, all right?"

Nate was mad as hell. He snatched his sweatshirt from the chair and looked at Alexis as if he could tear her to pieces. "You lucky they saved you this time. Next time, they won't be able to. Trust and believe that. I'm out."

"Me too," Theo said, grabbing a few more pieces of chicken and putting them into his pockets. He flipped his hoodie over his head and exited right behind Nate. I was getting ready to make a move too, until I saw Nate's daughter, Brianna, and her cousin standing by the doorway. Brianna had tears rolling down her face. Her cousin was trying to wipe them with a tissue. Seeing that shit took me back to where I didn't want to be. I looked at Alexis, as she pealed herself off the floor and eased in a chair. The bruise on her face was starting to darken—she wouldn't be able to hide it. No question, she was very beautiful, but as far as brains were concerned, she was lacking. To me, she had put up with Nate's shit for too long. But he was my boy, so I kept quiet about the shit. Especially when Brianna tried to comfort her mother, and she yelled for her to go to her room.

"Now, Brianna, and close the door! Take Jo with you!"

With a sad look on her face, Brianna did what she was told. I followed behind her and Jo, just to make sure they were okay.

"Who won the boxing match y'all were playing earlier?" I attempted to divert their attention elsewhere and make them forget about what they had witnessed or heard. They both claimed to be winners.

"You didn't win, Brianna. Stop lying," Jo said, then plopped on the bed and pouted.

"Yes, I did. I beat the pants off you, and you know it."

I teased Jo. "Man, you let a seven-year-old girl beat you? You'd better step up your game and get down to some for-real business with her."

Jo snatched the remote and turned on the TV. We all started to play the game, but this time Jo was winning. Brianna didn't like that, so she got mad and indulged herself even more in the game. She'd forgotten all about the argument between her parents, and by the time I left the room, they were laughing again.

I closed the door, then made my way to Nate and Alexis's bedroom. She was sitting on the edge of the bed, long, model-like legs crossed while scrolling through Facebook. Her tight jeans were unzipped, and with a half shirt on, nipples erect, I could tell she wasn't wearing a bra. I leaned against the doorway and eased my hands into my pocket.

"Can I get you anything before I go? I already know where Nate and Theo at, so I'ma go holla at him again about this. Maybe I'll be able to talk some sense into him, so don't worry about him coming back here, starting trouble."

Alexis lay the phone on the bed, then shifted her head in my direction. Her voice cracked as she spoke tearfully to me. "The only thing you can tell him is to come pack his things. I'm tired of this shit, Bones. Y'all just don't know how bad things really are. Tired of him putting his hands on me for no fucking reason at all."

She got up to blow her nose and looked at her bruised face in the mirror. While shaking her head, she moved her long hair behind her ears. "This is ridiculous. Last time, it was my lip. The time before that, it was my nose. And look at this right here. Trust me when I say you have no idea what kind of animal your friend is."

She came over to the doorway and lifted her shirt. Showed me two big-ass bruises near her breasts that looked like severe bite marks. She then moved her jeans away from her hip and showed me a bruise next to a heart tattoo with Nate's name scripted across it.

"He kicked me out of the bed last week and did this. Said I was snoring too loud, and he couldn't sleep. It's petty shit like that, that keeps setting him off. I honestly can't take this shit no more. Eventually, I'ma start fighting his ass back."

I released a deep sigh. I knew things were bad between them, and I feared that Nate would hurt her or she would hurt him. "Like I said . . . I'll talk to him, all right? Meanwhile, chill out and see about Brianna. He hasn't put his hands on her, has he?"

"No," Alexis said, biting her nails while standing in front of me. "He hasn't touched her, but it ain't like he gets any points for being a good dad. That nigga is a live-in deadbeat."

Sorry, I had to defend Nate. In actuality, he was the only one bringing money into the household. And as far as I knew, he did a whole lot for Brianna. He loved her, and he always talked about doing big things for his little girl.

"You may not know the real definition of a deadbeat," I said. "I can tell you this. It definitely ain't Nate."

Alexis rolled her eyes at me and professed that I was on the outside looking in. I kept trying to make my point, but it was as if she wasn't paying me much attention. Her eyes started to shoot me a seductive gaze. I would be lying if I said I hadn't seen that look in her eyes before. There was a possibility that Nate had seen it too. That was why he reacted the way he did. Her stare made me uncomfortable, so I quickly changed the subject.

"I'm getting ready to make a move. Put some ice on yo' face, and if or when Nate comes back, try not to go there with him."

As I stepped away from the door, Alexis reached for my bicep, squeezing it. "I need a *real* man in my life, Bones. I'm tired of messing around with little boys. You already know what's up, and one of these days, I want you, and only you, to rescue me from all of this bullshit."

I was never one to show my anger unless I had to. I wasn't sure what kind of game Alexis was playing, and I despised bitches who weren't loyal. This was a dangerous move. Alexis knew it.

"I rescued you once, and I won't do it again. I don't approve of how Nate treats you, but I'm starting to understand why my nigga can't control his actions."

She snickered at my comment and blew it off. And after taking a few steps back, she lifted her shirt over her head, exposing her breasts.

"Bones, you have things so twisted. I thought you, of all people, would be able to recognize your haters. If you think I'm one of them, you're sadly mistaken. At the end of the day, I'm on your side."

I didn't know that we needed to pick and choose sides. But I did know that something with Alexis was starting to stink real bad. She pressed her perky breasts against me, and as she brought her glossy lips to mine, I turned my head and stood there like stone. Rejection didn't play well with her, so she snatched my face and tried to force her tongue into my mouth. My face twisted, and I shoved her away from me.

"Back the fuck up," I said.

Her response was not anger, but persistence. She kept her eyes locked with mine as she paraded to the bedroom and stood by the bed. After dropping her jeans to the floor, she stood naked. Her near-perfect curves were a pretty sight to see—I couldn't lie. And so was her shaved pussy, when she sat back on the bed and opened her legs. She lifted her finger, motioning for me to come to her.

"Five minutes, Bones. All I need is a measly five *or* ten minutes of satisfaction. I promise to make every minute worth it. Afterward, you can go play with your boys."

I felt frozen in time. Couldn't help it that my eyes were glued to the prettiness of her pussy. Couldn't help that my dick was starting to rise, and I couldn't help that my anger and bad feelings about certain bitches was starting to grow.

"I'm disappointed," I said in a calm manner, displaying much seriousness, but trying my best to fight this. "Go fuck—"

Alexis halted my words when she slipped her fingers deep into her pussy and began to toy with herself. Her fingers were covered with a light glaze, and as her folds moved in and out, I released a deep breath. I didn't have much else to say, so I pivoted and headed for the door. I could hear Alexis's moans, and right after she spewed, "Bones, pleeease fuck me. I want you to fuuuck and suck this pussy so bad,"—I slammed the front door. My dick wasn't happy about me walking out, but I just couldn't betray my boy. I didn't have the guts to tell him about this incident either, only because I knew he would burn this muthafucking house down. The best thing he could do was rid himself of this slick bitch by leaving her.

RED

I hated how I made a living. But as any smart mutha-fucka would assume, stripping paid the bills. It didn't earn me much respect, though, but I seriously didn't give a fuck. I had to do something. Life hadn't always treated me well, and I'd been a street runner since I was thirteen.

I left the home where my father abused me and my mother allowed it. Never understood why people had kids, only to mistreat them. Could barely take care of them, and then got mad when they didn't want to accept the abuse. I mean, fuck my parents. I hadn't seen or spoken to them in years. They had given up on looking for me, and I damn sure wasn't looking for them. Now, this life was my happily ever after.

My first real gig came around my fourteenth birthday. I hooked up with two college niggas who had their way with me. They paid me a few hundred bucks that night, and when I realized how much I could let my pussy work for me, I turned to more niggas who were willing to pay. I didn't necessarily see it as a negative thing, until mutha-fuckas started disrespecting me. I'd been beat, slapped, kicked out of cars . . . You name it. Even thought about giving the shit up when I turned twenty-two, but the money was too good. By then, though, I had stepped up my game. Made some vital connections. I was hired at a well-known strip club that many celebrities and import-ant people frequented. Nobodies were allowed there too, but for the most part, I always left with big dollars in my pocket. Still, I hated the look of thirsty men who were willing to pay whatever, just to get a feel or a sniff of my pussy. I had minimized the niggas I actually had sex with, and the only reason I gave up the goodies was if I chose to. A nigga had to move me in a certain way, or he had better present me with some cash I couldn't resist.

As usual, the club was thick with thirsty niggas and curious women who came to see what was up. While I went by the name Red, my skin was chocolate and smooth. I wasn't like the other bitches around here, trying to look like Kim Kardashian with fake asses and hair extensions. My shit was all natural and was much appreciated by the men who couldn't get enough of seeing me. My curly, wild Afro bounced with each step that I took, and my deep-set eyes were dolled up with long lashes. I wore very little makeup on my flawless skin, but the shimmering, glittery lotion I rubbed all over me made me look like a million bucks. My lips were covered with gold gloss, and my curves were so perfect that the other strippers hated me. No one could touch the way I worked a pole, and my five-inch, crystal heels gave me much height so I could do one thing—look even sexier. I strutted around the club as if I owned it. With confidence in my eyes, as well as in my walk, many hungry eyes were locked on me.

While sliding the crack of my ass against a pole that was behind me, my eyes scanned the overly excited audience. Thick smoke clouded the space, disco balls turned from up above, and glass mirrors surrounded every inch of the club. Two bars were to the left and right, and the circular, marble floor was where most of the dancers started, but ended up working the crowd afterward. I had just gotten started and suddenly spotted a nigga I had set my eyes on a few months ago. I was extra horny that night and had given him the goodies for fifty bucks.

I loved and appreciated niggas who possessed good qualities before opening their mouths or wallets. There was something about him that moved me like no other. His hooded eyes were mysterious, sexy, serious as fuck, and luring. As he rocked my pussy to sleep that night, I stared into those eyes that made me melt with each stroke. There was a tiny cut above his smooth brow, and another one was right on his chin, where minimal fine hair covered it. He had a look that said, only if he wanted to, he knew how to tear some pussy up! He knew how to bring a bitch to her knees and make her crave for his big dick for a lifetime. He was packaged up very nicely, and as he gently fucked me in a stall that night, I was in a different zone. Normally, niggas were rough with me. He, however, took his time and stroked me like the same music was playing in both of our heads. Made me come all over him, but when it was over, he tossed the condom in the trash and smooth walked his way out the door. I hadn't seen or heard from him since.

I was so sure that he would return the next day or, at least, by the next week. But I hadn't seen him until tonight. He was sitting with a few other niggas, seeming to be indulged in a heavy conversation. He barely looked my way, and believe me when I say I was putting on quite a performance to capture his attention.

Maybe he'd forgotten about our little festivities that night. After all, I didn't give him my name, and he never told me his. When I attempted to kiss those thick, sexy lips, he turned his head to avoid me. I surely wanted to taste his tongue, but his dick had put on such a great performance that I didn't trip. I definitely thought about round two tonight, but then again, he appeared upset about something. He kept darting his finger as he spoke to the brother next to him, who, by the way, was called Nate. He came to the club quite often, along with the nerdy one who was kind of cute in his own little way. I wasn't sure what his name was, but the only one who had my full attention was Mr. Sexy. Even while rocking a simple white T-shirt, black jeans, and probably broke as shit, he still looked good and could get it at the snap of his finger.

"Turn around and make that pussy give us a smile," a rude white man shouted.

He and several of his friends were up close, celebrating something. Since it had been raining in their direction all night, I was kind to them. I put on my happy face, and when I bent over and separated my cheeks, several bills slapped my ass. Some dropped to the sticky, slick floor. I looked between my legs, noticing that the one I admired had pulled himself away from the conversation to take a glance too. Then, with the blink of an eye, he turned his head back to his friends and continued to talk. I needed more attention to swing my way, so like a sexy, runway model, I poked my breasts out and marched across the floor to a rapper and his entourage. They were pretty hyped too, and plenty of the light-bright bitches in the house were surrounding them, trying to get paid. They hated to see me coming, but just like that, my flawless brown skin sucked them all in. I squatted with my legs wide open, as I formed an arch in my back and grinded myself in circles; the niggas went crazy.

"I know you goin' home with me tonight. No questions asked," one member of the rapper's entourage said. Another claimed that I would, for sure, be leaving with him, but when one of the muthafuckas dissed me, I shortened my performance.

"Fuck that black bitch. That ho got an attitude, and she think she all that."

I smiled at the bastard and showed him my middle finger. I *was* all that. I proved it to him when his boys dropped big paper on me that night, and I walked away leaving them high and dry. I'd had enough of their filthy money, so I left the stage and began to work the crowd. Slowly but surely, I maneuvered my way over to the table where Nate was. They were still involved in a deep conversation, but all of them appeared to be more relaxed now. I sat on the table, then got on my hands and knees. I crawled to the sexy one who was at the head of the table, presenting himself as the one in control. His eyes were locked with mine. With his finger resting against his temple, along with a blank expression on his face, I couldn't tell if he was bored or not.

"Don't knock over my fucking drink," Nate spat with jealousy, as I crawled by him. He was so damn arrogant and rude, so I ignored him. I assumed he was having a bad night, because any other night, I couldn't keep his hands off me.

I approached the end of the table like a tiger looking for prey. Many men slapped my ass, touched it, paid to look at it, and then some.

"She a baaaaad muthafucka," someone said. "Damn!"

"I know. I come here all the time just to see Red work her magic."

I was face-to-face with the nigga who had the string between my pussy lips soaking wet. I clapped my ass, and when I smiled to show more of my pearly whites, he stood up.

"It's late," he said, shifting his eyes away from me. "Holla at you niggas tomorrow."

He gave everyone around him dap, and when the music changed, I picked up my cracked face and moved on to the next table. Minutes later, I saw Nate and his puppet leave too. I was damn sure disappointed that Mr. Sexy didn't recognize me, but what was more important than that was the money I had to make. I put aside my bruised feelings and resumed my business.

BONES

After I left the strip club, Nate and Theo followed. We stayed on the parking lot for a while, bringing our ongoing conversation to a close.

"I hear you loud and clear," Nate said. "And I promise you that I'ma chill. You know I don't make promises that I don't keep."

"Nigga, quit lying," Theo said, then yawned. "And whether you being truthful or not, you seriously need to keep yo' hands off that girl. If you ever do that shit again, just make sure my black ass ain't around to see it."

I reached out and slapped my hand against Theo's. I felt the same way. "That's what I'm saying. And even though I don't condone that shit, period, please make sure I'm at a distance. I don't have to tell you why seeing that disturbs me."

Nate nodded, and so did Theo. I figured they were thinking about how the shit went down when I was ten. We were all good friends at that time too, and I remember how badly they felt for me.

Theo yawned again, and then shielded his eyes with black-framed glasses that put him on nerd patrol. We always teased him about looking like Steve Urkel, but he didn't mind. According to him, his personality made up for it, and most chicks appreciated his charming ways.

"It's been a long day," he said. "I need to get home and into my bed, like now. If not, I'ma fall the hell to sleep on this concrete."

Theo rode with Nate and left his car at Nate's house. They jetted together, and right after they left, I went to my car. I checked my text messages when I got inside, and saw that my grandmother had sent me a message almost three hours ago about bringing her some Black Walnut ice cream. It was the least I could do, but before I headed to the grocery store, I sat in the car and finished the joint I had hit earlier. I slightly turned the ignition to let the rap music play, but when I attempted to start my car, it didn't budge. It was an old BMW that had given me its share of trouble in the past. This time, I chalked it up as the battery being fucked up because of the radio. I had a charger in the trunk, so I reached for it, then lifted the hood. I sat back in the car for a while, giving the charger time to give the battery some juice. I didn't have another joint to smoke, so I reached for my cigs in the glove compartment and lit one. I watched as many people from the club left, and others came. This was definitely the place to be, but like Theo, I was ready to get home and claim my comfortable bed.

A few more minutes had passed, so I figured the battery had been charged. I tapped my foot on the accelerator, but still nothing happened.

"Damn," I said, then sighed as I got out of the car and slammed the door. It had gotten kind of chilly outside, and the night breeze was cutting through my T-shirt. The cigarette dangled from my mouth as I looked under the hood to see what was wrong with my car. I couldn't see much, so I went back into the trunk to get a flashlight. I used it to see under the hood, and as soon as I heard several fools laughing, I turned my head.

"Do you bitches need a ride?" one of the white men said. He wasn't talking to me. He was talking to Red and another stripper who were walking a few feet in front of the man and his friends.

Red waved them off, but kept smiling. "No, thank you."

The other stripper didn't reply. She kept it moving, so the man rushed up to Red and grabbed her arm. The punk-ass security guard was standing right by the door. I couldn't believe that coward didn't do shit. I took a few more hits from the cigarette and watched.

"Release me," Red said as she attempted to jerk her arm away from the man. He was overly aggressive, and when he released her arm, he grabbed a chunk of her ass and squeezed it.

"Come here, you pretty bitch. Why are you ignoring us now?"

Red was trying to compromise with the man, but the other stripper kept telling her to come on. I knew a trouble-making fool when I saw one, and from where I was looking at it, Red was about to find herself in something she couldn't get out of.

I stepped away from my car and headed toward the scene that appeared to be turning ugly. "She said leave her the fuck alone," I said, then flicked my cigarette over to the side. The drunk, aggressive man ignored me, but the others stood back and didn't say shit.

"I can handle this fool," Red snapped at me, like I was the one who had done something to her. "Gon' about your business and move right along."

"Yeah," he slurred. "She can handle me, so take your ass back to your car and leave us the hell alone."

"Cool," I said, then turned around. The other stripper was already at her car, but seconds later, a glass bottle flew past me and crashed on the ground. I take it that the bottle was supposed to hit me, but missed. The drunk muthafucka laughed, but not for long. I charged at him, and before anyone knew it, I had him in a headlock with his arms twisted like a pretzel behind his back. The other dumb-ass fools, his friends I suspected, ran like bitches.

Red, however, asked me to be easy on her customer. The security guard didn't do shit but go back inside, pretending as if he hadn't seen a thing.

"Why you throw that bottle at me?" I twisted and turned the man's arm. He sobered up real quick and yelled how sorry he was.

"I . . . I was fucked-up, man. Fu . . . Forgive me, please."

Normally, I didn't let shit like this slide. I had to break something on this fool, so I opted for his wrist. I wrestled his hand back as far as it could go. He struggled to push back, but within a matter of seconds, his hand dangled off his wrist. He cried out and ran off, holding it in front of him. I was so irritated by the fool that I chased after him and punted him in the ass with my foot.

"Really?" Red barked as she watched the man running faster to get away from me. "Did you have to go that far? He was one of my good-paying customers, and you done fucked up my money."

When bitches talked silly shit, I ignored them. Walked right past her without saying a word. She followed behind me as I went to my car and attempted to start it again. No luck.

"Fuck," I said, hitting the steering wheel. I looked at Red who had a smirk on her face.

"Car trouble, huh? I guess you'll be needing a ride."

I could have called Nate to come back and get me, but what the hell? "If it's not a problem," I said.

"No problem, especially since you out here protecting me and everything. You broke the shit out of his wrist. How'd you do that so fast?"

Wasn't my fault if she wasn't watching. "I was protecting myself. Not you."

I closed the hood and locked up my car. Red's car was parked at the side of the building where there weren't many lights. There was a nearby exit door too. I wondered why she hadn't used it.

"Before you ask, the owner has chains on that door so nobody can slip inside. The front entrance is the only way in and the only way out."

I shrugged, then got inside of her car. Before driving off, she put a brown paper bag in the glove compartment, and then looked in the rearview mirror to slide some gloss on her lips.

"Where do you live?" she said. "I hope not far because I do not feel like stopping to get gas."

"I'll put my address in your GPS device. You'll definitely have to stop to get gas, and I need for you to stop at the grocery store too."

She tied a colorful silk scarf around her wild hair, then responded to my request. "Nigga, you got some gas money? And I assure you that I won't be stopping at no grocery store."

I reached for my wallet and opened it to flip through my cash. Unfortunately, I only had seven dollars to my name. I had a little more cash at home, but if I offered her gas money, then I wouldn't be able to get my grandmother her ice cream.

"This all I got." I showed her the seven dollars. "Maybe I can give you an IOU."

"I don't accept IOUs, and how you gon' come to a strip club with seven measly dollars in your pocket?"

Red drove off and followed the directions I'd put into her GPS device. "I didn't come here tonight for that kind of action. Came to holla at my boys."

"Yeah, whatever. I got you covered tonight, but if you ever want to ride with me again, having gas money is a must."

I shut my eyes and laid my head back on the headrest. "Good thing I won't ever have to ride with you again then."

Red didn't respond. If she did, I didn't hear her. I dozed off and didn't crack my eyes open until we got to the gas station. The least I could do was pay, with her money, and pump the gas. I held out my hand, but all she did was look at it.

"What?" she said.

"I need money to pay for gas. I showed you all that I had on me."

She said something smart underneath her breath, and then reached for the brown bag she'd put in the glove compartment. I also saw a gun in there. It was good to know that she was smart enough to protect herself. She counted out forty dollars, then placed it in my hand.

"There. Bring me some gum and a diet Pepsi too. Also, if they have some of those chewy things . . . you know, those gummy bears in there, bring me some of those as well."

I didn't bother to reply to her nonsense. I went inside to pay for the gas, and luckily for me, I was able to find a box of Black Walnut ice cream for my grandmother. It cost me $5.99, plus tax, so I didn't have enough for the extra stuff Red requested. Her forty dollars was pumped into the tank. When I got back into the car, she reached for the bag with the ice cream in it.

"Thanks," she said. "Did you find the gummies?"

"Nope. I didn't have enough to pay for your stuff. In the bag is ice cream for my grandmother."

Her mouth dropped wide open. "Nigga, are you serious? That ice cream will melt by the time we get to your grandmother's house. And in case you don't know this, my car doesn't have taxi written all over it. I'm only taking you to your crib. Not anywhere else."

"Great. My home is at my grandmother's house. Let's roll so I can get her ice cream to her."

Red pursed her lips. "Aww, hell, nah. You live with your grandmother? For whatever reason, I thought you had it . . . never mind. As they say, never judge a book by its cover."

"So, now, you're insulting me, right? A few months ago, you were bent over in that bathroom stall with glee in yo' eyes and looking as if you wanted to break down, cry, and tell me how much you loved me."

Her neck started to roll. I'm sure I pushed her buttons with that one. "Nigga, please don't flatter yourself. And I'm surprised you remembered *that night*. You acted as if you didn't even remember me."

I closed my eyes again and licked across my lips. "Yeah, I remember. I keep remembering to forget."

Red lightly pushed my shoulder, then left me at peace. I slept the entire way home, and when she parked in my driveway, she woke me up.

"Is this where you live?" she asked.

I looked at our small, red brick house with no lights on. My grandmother didn't play when it came to her light bill, and she minimized electricity as much as she could. "Yeah, this is me. Thanks for the ride. I promise not to inconvenience you again."

"I hope not, but, uh, before you go, are you gon' tell me your name or not? I guess you know my name is Red, but you still haven't told me your name."

"Why does it matter? Especially since I'm a broke, troublemaking, granny's boy who you thought could meet your standards."

"You don't, but I still want to know your name."

I hesitated to tell her anything. "Bones. My name is Bones."

"Quit lying. That shit is funny, but I'm not in the mood to laugh."

I opened the car door, but Red grabbed my arm to stop me. She snapped her finger. "Okay, I get it. They call you Bones because you like to break things, right?

Like you broke that man's wrist back there at the club. Again, you shouldn't have done that. He was really a nice guy, just an asshole when he's sloppy drunk."

"Whatever. Look, I'm real tired. Don't want my grandmother's ice cream to melt either. Call me whatever you wish, and thanks for the ride."

"Can I call you tomorrow? If you give me your number, I'll call you when I get off work tomorrow. Maybe we can hook up for a late dinner or something."

Red was trouble. I could smell it. Shit was written all over her. Our conversation was good, though. Just not good enough. "I'll pass. Again, thanks for the ride and be safe going home."

This time, she didn't stop me when I made a move. And by the time I made it to the door, she had pulled out of the driveway and drove off. I put the key in the door and went inside. I could barely see, so I turned on an old-fashioned lamp in the living room. My grandmother's house was outdated, but spotless. She kept things real tidy, and there weren't too many things that were out of place. I went into her bedroom where she lay sound asleep. I could hear her snores, so I bent down and planted a soft kiss on her cheek. I put her ice cream in the freezer, expecting that she would get to it in the morning when she woke up.

BONES

The next morning, I was up early, fixing my car. All I needed was a new battery, and I already had one in the garage. It needed charging too, and I was relieved when the ignition turned over. I drove off the parking lot and got on my way to search for a new job. I was willing to accept anything that put change in my pockets. But as I sat at a hardware store, filling out an application for a janitorial position, I changed my mind. I crumbled the application in my hand and walked out. After hearing how the supervisor spoke to the other workers, and when he told me the job was only paying minimum wage, I knew this wasn't the place for me. Theo called as I was getting in the car. He immediately heard the frustration in my voice.

"I'm not trying to push you to do the wrong thing, but it ain't no fun being broke. There are plenty more ways for you to get your hands on money, and just like the rest of us, sometimes, you gotta do what you gotta do, until something else better comes along."

"Something else like what?"

"Like go see that nigga Mango. See if he'll hook you up with something. After you distribute that shit, give him his cut and keep yours. The police don't be tripping like you think they do. And all you have to do is keep a low profile and create some regular customers. If need be, I can loan you some money to get by. But you gotta start puttin' that petty shit behind you and be willing to make moves to the next level. Meanwhile, don't tell Mango I sent you his way, and don't tell him that you've seen me. He be acting funny sometimes, but don't take it personal."

I suspected that Theo and Nate were sick of me borrowing money. And it wasn't fair to them that they were the ones taking risks, and I wasn't. I decided to take his advice and go see Mango.

Within the hour, I sat at a kitchen table with Mango. He was an old cat with a twitching eye, a meaty baldhead, and a potbelly that boiled over his sweats. Nappy beads of hair were on his bare chest, but diamond rings were on every last one of his fingers. Two of his henchmen sat close by on a leather sectional, watching my every move. Several chicks were on the couch too, and one of them winked at me from afar. I paid her no attention, and I listened to Mango speak to me as if I wasn't shit. He knew that I needed his help, and that caused him to turn up the heat.

"I don't know what took you so long to come here. You thank you better than me and the other niggas around here? And when did you thank it was okay for you to go work for the white man instead of the black man? I pay a whole lot better than he does, and any muthafucka who don't realize that is just plain ol' stupid in my opinion."

I wiped my mouth just to silence myself. This nigga had done nothing but insult me, but I remained calm. I guess too calm for him, because he continued to push.

"So now, you've come here to beg me to help you. To be truthful, I don't trust niggas with yo' reputation with my goods."

With that being said, I stood to go. Coming here was a waste of time. I'd heard enough.

"Sit the fuck down," Mango shouted. "I'm not done talkin' to you yet, and while I don't trust you with my goods, I would like to utilize yo' talents in another way. Do want you to consider doing some other things for me?"

I reluctantly eased back down in the chair to listen. Mango placed a stack of hundreds on the table, fanning them out in front of me.

"Two thousand dollars ain't a bad pay for a day's work. And from what I've heard, a nigga like you can be very beneficial to me. I like how you keep yourself in control, like you are right now. That shit is impressive."

He reached behind him, then laid a photo on the table. While sucking his teeth, he eased the photo over to me. "I need to brang that nigga some for-real pain. He's been tripping with my money, and he needs what I refer to as a wake-up call. Don't want him dead—too valuable to me. Just want him hurt. My men over there are only killers. They don't like to scare people, but I hear that you do. Why don't you take this money, find that nigga for me today, and bring me back something as a souvenir. I'll let you decide what that will be. If things work out, I have some other *jobs* I'd like for you to take care of for me too."

I cracked my knuckles and bit down on my bottom lip. Even though this shit sounded like it was up my alley, I still wasn't so sure. I stared at the money, thinking how badly I needed it. I could give some of it to my grandmother to help her out, but not all of it because she'd grow suspicious. Either way, I hadn't had that much money in my possession, at once, for a long time.

"I'll do it," I said. "You'll have your souvenir soon."

Mango nodded, and for the first time, displayed a crooked smile. He rolled up the money and slapped it right in my hand. "I hope I can count on you," he said. "Ain't too many niggas like you left around here. I always knew that you were kind of . . . special."

I didn't respond. I knew what he meant, because the streets talked. Talked about me and about my *abilities* as a bone crusher. I dreamed about one day working for the CIA, being a spy or being on some James Bond shit. Never did I suspect that I would be utilizing my *talents* in this way.

Mango provided me with a key location where this nigga, Quinton, could be found. But before going on my search, I went home to kick my grandmother out with some paper. She was sitting at the dining room table watching *The Price Is Right* and eating her ice cream. Foam rollers were tightened around her gray hair, and she was still in her pink nightgown. Her chocolate skin had very few wrinkles, and for a sixty-eight-year-old woman, she still looked good.

"You were up early," she said as I came into the dining room. "And take that hoodie off your head. Look like you be up to something when you have that thing over your head like that."

I pulled the hoodie off my head, then reached into my pocket. I laid $900 on the table and lied my ass off. "I got paid yesterday. Cashed my check this morning, right after I had to go fix my car. It stopped on me last night."

"Did you have enough money to fix it?"

"Yep. It wasn't nothing but the battery."

"Good. Now move yo' tail out of the way so I can see if this woman gon' win a car. I like to see people win, especially the black folks."

I laughed and went into the kitchen where she had fried some bacon, scrambled eggs, and made some hash browns. After pouring my orange juice, I sat at the table to eat.

"Why you eating ice cream for breakfast and you cooked this?"

"Because I needed some dessert. I know this ol' diabetic body of mine don't want me to have it, but you know I gotta have my ice cream and sweet potato pies. If you think about it later, pick me up one of those pies from that soul food joint I like. Then again, never mind. I'ma drive to get me some chicken later. I'll stop then."

I chewed my eggs, then swallowed. "Now, you know you shouldn't be out there driving, especially since you always complaining about how much you can't see."

"I can see where the chicken house is, and I damn sure know how to make my way back home. If somebody get in my way, too doggone bad."

My grandmother was a trip. She was sweet as pie, though, and was, without a doubt, the only person I had ever loved.

I finished breakfast, then headed to my bedroom. It was a ten-by-nine foot small room with a full-sized bed and dresser. A black rug covered the polished hardwood floors and several crooked pictures of me with my grandmother were on the wall. I also had a picture of me and Mama too. It was in my drawer. The entire room was simple but clean. My bed was already made, thanks to my grandmother, and the smell of Lysol infused the air. There was no question that I could've found a place of my own, but for whatever reason, I just didn't want to leave her. The only person she had was me. The only person I had was her. Living separate didn't make sense, and to hell with what any bitch thought of me. Until she left this earth, I would be right here.

I quickly changed into my Adidas sweat suit and tennis shoes. Brushed my waves, stroked the minimal hair on my chin, then trimmed my mustache. My chocolate skin was always so smooth, and I had to do very little to enhance my appearance. I placed a white cap on my head, then put my cigs in my pocket. After that, I said good-bye to my grandmother and pursued my first mission.

RED

I didn't like Nate, but as always, money talks. He was in my bedroom, attempting to fuck my brains out, but failed. With each hard thrust, my head banged into the headboard in front of me. The mattress squeaked loudly, and the smell of sex infused the air. I pretended that the sex was all that—didn't want to hurt his feelings. I was very good at faking orgasms to make a nigga feel good.

Our bodies dripped with sweat. And after so long, the room got stuffy. Nate kept smacking my ass so hard that it stung.

"What you got to say about that shit?" he said between deep breaths. "Told you I was gon' tear this shit up, didn't I?"

I sucked in my bottom lip. "Yeah, you did, baby. You've made a believer out of me!" *Yeah, right*, I thought. The only reason I let Nate come over was because he called and told me he had a proposition for me. One that I wouldn't be able to refuse. He hadn't said much about it yet, only that it involved someone I knew. In the meantime, he needed a good fuck. He paid, and I delivered.

He got his; I pretended to get mine. We lay next to each other exhausted. He could barely catch his breath—I watched as his chest heaved in and out. I then reached on the nightstand for a cigarette. After I lit it, I took a long drag, then whistled smoke into the air. I glanced at the clock on the nightstand, seeing that it was almost 6:00 p.m.

"What's on your mind, Nate? I need to get a nap before I go to work tonight."

Nate turned on his side, then reached for my chin, rubbing it. "While that pussy was worth every penny that I'm giving you, I need for you to do me a favor."

"It depends on what it is and who it involves."

"It involves a good friend of mine. I've noticed your interest in him, and I can't think of a better person than you to handle this little situation for me."

I smashed the cigarette in the ashtray, then turned sideways to look at him. "I'm listening. You have my full attention."

"Bones. I want you to do whatever to bring that nigga to his knees, and I do not only mean that by sucking his dick. I need you to weaken him. Make him love you like he has loved no other. Make him want you and not be able to function without you. And then when you get him to that point, I want you to, well, kill him."

I cocked my head back and frowned. "*Kill* him? Maybe I can do all of that other shit for you, but I don't kill people. Besides, I kind of like Bones. He's fine as fuck, sexy as shit, and I must say that his dick performs waaaay better than yours."

I was only kidding, then again, I wasn't. Either way, Nate didn't appreciate my playfulness. He grabbed my face and squeezed my cheeks so hard that I couldn't turn my head.

"Don't play with me, bitch, all right? This shit is serious! That nigga did some foul shit to me, been keeping secrets, and I'm willing to do whatever to make sure he pays for it. A fine bitch like you need to act on this and get that paper for helping me out."

He released his grip, then attempted to apologize. "I didn't mean to shake you up like that, but I need you. Bones is real smart. He senses certain things about people, so you gotta be careful. He's always watching his back, but you can do this. I saw the way he eyed you last night. He's feeling you, trust me. I know you're the only one who can catch him off guard, and without him suspecting anything, help me bring him to his demise."

Niggas were a trip. They were always plotting and scheming. I assumed these fools were real close, then again, what did I know?

"I don't know what you think you saw in his eyes last night, but I can tell you right now that that nigga ain't feeling me. He had car trouble last night. I drove him home. I inquired about hooking up with him, and he rejected me. Plus, you saw how he did me at the club. I'm not going to keep putting myself out there for a nigga who ain't interested. In conjunction with all of that, let me remind you, again, that I'm not a killer."

"Okay, I'll do the killing. All you have to do is drug him and leave the rest to me. And before you respond to that, answer this. How does twenty Gs sound?"

I cocked my head back and smiled. "Twenty thousand dollars? For real? And all I have to do is drug him? Nigga, don't play."

"That's it. Keep quiet about this, drug him, and then call me."

There really wasn't much else to think about. I liked Bones, no doubt. But I loved money. I held out my hand and looked at Nate. "Put up or shut up. When do I get paid?"

"Five now, the rest later. I need to see you making progress. I'll know if you have, if and when that nigga starts talking about you. If he kisses you, you're in there. And if he tells you his real name, love is definitely in his heart."

"I can guarantee you that he will, but just for the hell of it, what *is* his real name?"

"Can't say. It'll be yo' job to find out."

I winked at Nate, and only because I was hyped about the money, I gave that nigga another taste of my sweet pussy.

BONES

I had been casing the streets for at least three hours trying to find Quinton. I didn't want to ask anyone if they'd seen him, only because I had to stay low-key. Niggas were already eyeing me like I was the police. I was in a hood that wasn't familiar to me, but I still managed to see some of the fellas I once hung around with.

Being thirsty, I went into a convenience store to get an energy drink. I grabbed a pack of powdered donuts too, and on my way out, I received a text message from Theo. He asked how things went between me and Mango. Instead of texting him back, I called him.

"That fool wasn't trying to help me." I lied because Mango asked me not to speak a word about my new job to anyone. I felt as if it was in my best interest to keep this between us. "I wasted my damn time."

"Damn, sorry to hear that. I just knew he'd hook you up, but, uh, if you still need to get that paper, let me know."

"I'm good. I got hired today cleaning floors at a church. The pastor wants me to strip and wax them tomorrow. He paid me some advance money that should carry me for a minute."

"That day-by-day shit ain't about nothing. Me and Nate gon' hit up a few houses in the suburbs tonight. Found out about two families who are vacationing in Florida. Ain't nobody there but the dogs. Word is they got some good shit in there. Let us know before midnight if you down."

I didn't hesitate. I was sure this was something that Theo didn't want to hear. "I can tell you right now that I won't be rolling with y'all. Be easy and hit me up when you niggas get done."

"Will do, but you know where we'll be."

I spotted a dude who kind of fit Quinton's description. I quickly told Theo that I would catch up with them later. I watched as the dude pumped some gas, then jetted. Following closely behind him, I leaned down in my seat and began to take a few hits from my cig. Dude seemed to be constantly checking his rearview mirror, so I merged off to the right as if I was going elsewhere. I had a potential address for him. It appeared he was moving in that direction, even though he wasn't at that address earlier.

I circled the streets for a while, and then from a distance, I saw Quinton park his car in a complex heavy with a bunch of welfare recipients. The tall brick buildings looked as if they were ready for demolition. Windows were broken, laundry swung from several of the balconies, and plenty of unkempt-looking kids were running around. Loud mouths could be heard a mile away, and two chicks outside looked as if they were gearing up to fight. Quinton stopped to say something to one of the chicks, and that's when I saw him pass her a bag of weed. She smiled, and then got back to arguing with the chick who stood before her. When Quinton walked off to go inside, I got out of my car. I moved swiftly to catch him at the elevator.

As we both got on the elevator, he glanced at me, and then hit the eighth floor. I moved over to the left, as if I was on my way up to the eighth floor too. The squeaky elevator closed, and as the smell of piss gave my nose a tingle, I winced. Quinton had his hands in his pockets, and then he closed his eyes.

"Nigga, what you want with me?" he said, then opened his eyes to look across the elevator at me. "I saw you following me. What's up?"

He raised his sweatshirt so I could see his Glock secured in the front of his sagging jeans. I shrugged and played clueless.

"I don't know what you talking about. I wasn't following you; you must be paranoid about something. I'm here to see a friend of mine."

"What's yo' friend's name?"

"None of yo' damn business."

He reached for his gun, but in a matter of seconds, I snatched it from him and slapped him across the face with the butt of it. The elevator doors parted, and I hurried to toss the gun into the hallway. Quinton held his busted up face and tried to rush from the elevator to get his gun. Either he was too slow, or, most likely, I was too fast. I tangled his feet with mine, causing him to trip and fall flat on his face. The elevator closed again. We wrestled, but he was no match. I positioned him on his stomach and pressed my knee into his back.

"What in the fuck do you want from me?" he yelled. "Who the fuck are you, nigga?"

I pulled his arms behind his back and positioned them into a tight X. His movements caused my grip to be more painful, so he finally lay still.

"What I want is simple. Handle yo' business with Mango. He's waiting for you."

Never wasting time with a lot of talk, I did what I knew best and twisted Quinton's arm so tight that his bone snapped and popped through his skin. His loud scream echoed in the elevator, and he hollered so loud that I had to silence him. I released his arms, then slammed him in the mouth with my powerful, balled-up fist. His lip busted wide open—the white meat was on display.

Blood gushed from his lips, but I still reached into his bloody mouth to collect my souvenir. With a tight grip on one of his many rotten teeth, I pulled and yanked that muthafucka clean from his mouth. By then, he was in a daze. In shock. Speechless. The elevator opened, and a chick stood with groceries in her hand. Her eyes bugged as she saw Quinton lying there, looking deformed. She didn't know if he was dead or alive. Her bags hit the floor, and she screamed. I stepped over Quinton, excused myself, and made my exit.

I sped off the parking lot, and within thirty minutes, I was back at the table with Mango. He smiled at the bloody tooth I put on the table for him to see; as promised, my work had been done.

"You did good," he said, standing and massaging my shoulders. "I knew I was gon' like you."

I shrugged my shoulders as a gesture for him to move his hand. Didn't appreciate him touching me, but I didn't want to say it. He cleared his throat while standing in front of me, rubbing his hands.

"Based on what one of my boys said he witnessed, I think we gon' work well together. If anybody questions you, you don't know nothing, you ain't seen nothing, and you wasn't there. I already have the cops under control, so no need to worry. These niggas out here need to understand that business is business. You can't play with a man's money. For now, go celebrate yo' good deed. Have some fun tonight. I'll probably need yo' services again by the weekend, especially if this fool tries to disappear."

I nodded, and as Mango held out his hand, I slammed mine against his. Afterward, I left to go see what was up with Nate and Theo at the club. They were already there chilling and having drinks with several other dudes. Theo was there with his main chick, Nichelle. I was surprised to see Alexis there too. I guessed she wasn't tired anymore.

"It's about damn time," Nate said, standing as I approached the table. We gave each other dap; then I sat to the right of him while Alexis remained to his left. Nichelle was sitting on Theo's lap. He cocked his head back to acknowledge my presence.

Several drinks were already on the table, and there was also a cake. "Who or what are we celebrating tonight?"

"Don't you see my name on the cake?" Alexis said in a sassy tone. "It's my birthday, duhhh."

I nodded, then looked at the cake and saw her name. I didn't say anything yet, 'cause today seemed like a good day for Alexis. She had her man by her side, and I hoped she was happy about that. Theo and Nichelle had been together for a long time too. He had his doggish ways, no doubt, but Nichelle had his heart. She was nothing like Alexis, and I had much respect for Nichelle.

I looked past Nate to get at Alexis. "Happy Birthday, ma. Enjoy the night."

She smiled, and then wrapped her arms around Nate's neck. "I most certainly will. Especially since I just got my birthday present from my man."

She bragged about a diamond necklace that Nate had gotten her. I wasn't hating at all, but I couldn't believe how simple some hoes were. If diamonds made a muthafucka forget about being battered, so be it. She was definitely confused, but I was staying out of it.

They kissed as if love lived right at their front door. I looked away, and that's when I saw Red working the floor, doing her thing. I had hoped to avoid her tonight, but after I had several drinks, she sashayed her way over by us.

"I can't stand that bitch," Alexis whispered to Nichelle. "She always up in niggas' faces, thinking she the finest thing on earth."

Nate cleared his throat, then snapped at Alexis. "Chill with that shit tonight. We here to have fun, not hate on muthafuckas."

I wasn't sure if Red heard Alexis or not, but I sensed some tension between them. Alexis kept rolling her eyes, and for whatever reason, Nichelle got up from the table and walked away. She was one person who didn't like drama. A couple of females, and several brothas, gave Red all the attention she needed.

Nate reached over and patted my chest with the back of his hand. "What you think about that?" he said, referring to Red. "She fine, ain't she? And I know you gon' hit that again."

I shrugged. "Maybe, maybe not. She ain't really my type though."

"What? Since when? You have always appreciated the brown skin, and ain't nothing on her fake. Plus, the last time I checked, you don't fuck bitches who don't excite you. Obviously, something about her intrigues you."

I turned to glance at Red, admitting to myself that there was something about her that I liked. Still, and not trying to judge her, but I wasn't feeling what she did for a living. The way she was putting herself out there was enough to make any nigga involved with her mad.

Alexis cleared her throat before I responded to Nate. "I don't appreciate you sitting here talking about how fine this bitch is. And shame on yo' nasty ass, Bones, for fucking her. Ugh," she said, then got up from the table. She stormed off and knocked a few chairs out of her path.

"That bitch acts like she be on her period twenty-four-seven," Nate said. "She be itching for me to knock her ass out. I'm trying hard not to go there with her on her birthday."

"Try harder. For once, let's have some fun and not trip off things that we have no control over."

Nate nodded and clinked his glass with alcohol in it against mine. As soon as my glass was cleared, Red made her way up to me. She stood behind me, rubbing my chest and moving her hand down low to touch my package. I squeezed her hand to stop her.

"Awww," she teased, then bent over to whisper in my ear. "I promise I won't hurt it."

My boys laughed; I didn't. And when Red swung around me to deliver a lap dance, I stood up. I flipped a quarter on the table and looked directly in her eyes.

"All I got is change. And with all of these bills waving in the air, I suggest that you go get them and not waste yo' time on me."

I could see the fire in Red's eyes. She was pissed. Feelings hurt. She cut her eyes at me, then strutted away to go collect the rest of her money.

"Damn, nigga," Theo said, then laughed. "That was hard—some cold shit. Bitch working that hard, and all you can up with is a quarter?"

Nate replied too. "You know how Bones is. Shouldn't surprise you."

I silenced both of those fools when another stripper came by, shaking her ass and teasing me by displaying the long length of her tongue. I eased a fifty-dollar bill between her legs, then planted a soft kiss on her thigh.

"Thank you, sugga," she said, then winked. "Baby doll appreciates your generosity."

I bobbed my head to the music, watching her as she moved on to the next. Nate questioned my actions.

"Don't tell me you feelin' her better than you are Miss Red. If so, I can hook you up."

I shot Nate a look that he probably deemed offensive. "No offense, but, uh, why you so adamant about me and Red hooking up? You done said her name about fifty times tonight, and I'm starting to relate to and understand Alexis's concerns. If you want to hook up with her, nigga, please do. She's all yours, 'cause I don't want it."

Nate's eyes grew wide. He appeared shaken by my tone, but I was tired of the nigga bugging.

"From here on out," he said, pretending to zip across his lip, "my lips are sealed about Red. I ain't interested in that slut, especially since it's obvious that she's interested in you."

I remained silent. Nate and I had our issues before, but nothing major. I felt as if we all were starting to grow apart, only because I wasn't down with some of the things him and Theo did. They had already robbed those two houses tonight, and couldn't stop bragging about all the shit they'd gotten. To me, it didn't compare to the new gig I had, and when all was said and done, I expected to have more paper than any of us could dream of.

"Boo, I'm ready to go," Nichelle said to Theo. He had given her a few of the credit cards he'd stolen earlier and invited her to have at it. I assumed she was ready to go shopping.

"Holla at y'all later," I said, giving Nichelle a hug, then sending Theo off with a pound. Nate gave his good-byes too, and with Alexis still being mad, she only mumbled good-bye.

"I'ma go drain the vein, and then we gon' leave too," Nate said. "You staying or what?"

"Not sure yet. Maybe so."

The minute he left the table, Alexis moved in the chair next to me. "I wanted to apologize for the other night," she said. "I don't know what got into me. I got carried away. But the one thing I won't do is deny my feelings. Now you know how I feel. I honestly do not love Nate anymore, and I—"

I quickly silenced her. My face twisted, and I hated that she kept swinging this bullshit my way.

"If you don't love him anymore, then tell that nigga what's up! Stop putting me in the middle of this shit, expecting me to say something to him. If that's your plan, try again. I don't give a fuck how you feel, 'cause at the end of the day, ain't nothin' happening between you and me."

"Then why are you so mad? You are so good at pretending that you don't care, but I know you, Bones. I watch you, and I know—"

"Yeah, and I know you too. And the one thing that I know for sure is, if you don't back the fuck up and stop talking this shit, I'ma lay yo' ass out on this floor. I'm sure Nate won't appreciate my actions, but you ain't leaving me with many choices."

Alexis took heed to my warning. She knew I was a doer, not a talker.

She swung her long hair back, then plopped back into her seat. Giving a toast to herself, she picked up the glass of alcohol. "Happy Fucking Birthday to me." She guzzled the liquid down, then slammed the glass on the table. "What a fucked-up night. Yo' ass sitting here with an attitude, and that ho-ass nigga of mine can't stay out of these bitches' faces. I'm sick and tired of the goddamn disrespect."

There she go with that shit again. I swear I wanted to knock the fuck out of her. But since her attention was now on Nate, I passed. She wasn't playing with him tonight. As he stood whispering in another chick's ear, Alexis walked up to him and smashed his face with a huge chunk of her birthday cake. She embarrassed the fuck out of him, especially when she also slapped his face with a beer can that busted open and splashed all over him. Plenty of people laughed, and as many shook their heads, he pulled Alexis by her hair, dragging her out of the club. As always, the security guards didn't do shit. I wanted to intervene, but I kept thinking . . . That's what her ass gets.

"He shouldn't be doing her like that," one chick said. "That's a damn shame!"

"She's the one who started it," another said, defending Nate's actions. "That was on her."

"Wrong is wrong, and a man should never put his hands on a woman."

I agreed, but only to a certain extent. I listened to all of the opinions, but had come to my own conclusion. Both of them were wrong. They deserved each other.

I stayed for a while longer. Mingled with the ladies and kicked it with the fellas. By the time I left, rain was pouring down. I pulled my cap down further to cover my waves, and when I got to my car, Red stood by the driver's door, soaking wet. Her breasts were clearly visible through the thin shirt. It clung to her body, showing her hard nipples. The short skirt did nothing to prevent rain from wetting her legs, and her face was drenched.

"You are not going to believe this," she said, squinting and blinking rain from her long lashes. "I got a flat tire. I was getting ready to go back inside, but then I saw you coming."

"You're right. I don't believe you. Quit tripping and go home."

I politely moved Red away from my door, causing her to stumble a bit in her high heels.

"Playing? I'm serious!" she shouted. "I helped you, and you damn well better help me."

I didn't like her tone. Yelling at me wasn't going to help her in no way. "Bring it down or else. Show me this flat tire, and for your sake, I hope you ain't lying."

Red sighed and walked away. I cautiously followed and turned my head in many directions, closely observing my surroundings. I could see her car from a short distance, but as we walked past the building, Red veered to the right. She stood next to the building where I could barely see her.

"Come here," she said softly. "I want to show you something."

"The only thing you'd better be showing me is a flat tire."

"I'll show you that in a minute. For now, stop being so afraid of me and come here. Why you keep on trying to be so hard?"

In no way was I afraid of Red, and after all that had happened to me, I didn't have to pretend to be hard. Thing is, I wasn't sure what the fuck she was up to. It was still raining hard, and her ass was out here playing games. I stepped forward and saw her unbuttoning her shirt. She then dropped her skirt to her ankles. No panties. No nothing, but a whole lot of Hershey's beautiful chocolate.

"Forgive me. I'm a liar." Her tone softened again. "My car is fine, but I still need your help. I can't stop thinking about you fucking me again. In order for my urge to go away, I need to feel you deep inside of me. If I have to beg you not to walk away, I will. I will get on my knees and do whatever you want me to do."

This bitch was crazy. Crazy as fuck. But as she slowly kneeled and began to massage herself with gobs of mud, my muthafucking ass got turned on. I didn't dare move—the only thing moving was my dick growing to new heights. Water dripped from the brim of my hat, so I squinted to watch her unique performance. I damn sure didn't want anyone to interrupt, so I moved closer to the building that was now blocking me. Red stood, then came to me with a condom dangling from the corner of her mouth. She backed me against the wall, and then yanked my sweats down to my ankles. My hard dick slapped her in the face, but she laughed as she used her mouth to ease the condom on. Her sucks were very intense. Soft, then hard. Deep, then deeper. My dick shaved against the back of her throat, and my legs buckled when she almost swallowed all of me. I tore my jacket away from my chest. Pulled my T-shirt over my head. My cap was tossed in the mud, and as my lengthy steel was thrusting fast in and out of her mouth, damn near knocking any and all plaque from her teeth, I was almost defeated. My legs weakened. I jerked myself back to prevent myself from firing off.

Like a slithering snake, Red pressed her muddy body against mine. My dick was ready for some more action, and as I lifted her to my hips, my weak knees wouldn't allow me to hold her. We slipped, fast. I did my best to secure her in my arms, but we still landed in the muddy puddle behind us. Red laughed, then wrapped her soft, long legs around my back.

"Shame on you," she said, appearing to enjoy herself. "Look at what you did."

"I ain't done nothing yet. But I'm getting ready to."

She threw her arms around my broad shoulders, and as I positioned my dick at the moist entrance of her hole, I finally cracked the code. She gasped. Moaned. Held her breath, and latched her pussy on to me so I wouldn't move at a fast pace. I already suspected that I was too much for her to handle. By the third or fourth stroke, she formed a high arch in her back and squeezed her eyes together. She bit into her lip, then started to slowly grind her hips. To my rhythm. My beat. One that I was sure she could hang with.

"Mmmmmm, Bones, you just don't know how this feeeeeeels. My pussy has been wanting, needing, craving you for a loooong time. Looooong time, but I'ma need—"

I crept my hand over her mouth to quiet the noise. This was my show. I damn sure didn't need a woman to tell me how to make my moves. I removed Red's arms from my neck, then lifted her slippery legs over my shoulders. I could feel mud rolling down my back, but the heavy rain quickly washed it away. My dick was pushed in as far as it could go, stuffing her pussy to full capacity. She could barely catch her breath. I pressed her knees against her chest and began to grind and thrust faster inside of her. She grunted. Screamed. Whined.

"Ooooh, shit . . . Please, please, help me. My pussy can't take this beating. I . . . I'm about to cooooommme."

I helped her sweet juices flow by tickling her clit with the tips of my fingers and pounding into her cage simultaneously. Her nipple was in my mouth, and her hands massaged the solid muscles all over my now-muddy body. I felt her legs shaking on my shoulders; then they dropped into the puddle. We were caught up in the moment. She breathed in, I breathed out. Our gaze was locked. She then lifted her head, attempting to kiss me. I rejected it.

"I want to taste your tongue," she moaned.

I moved my head from side to side, then reached for her arm. "Turn around," I said. "We ain't done yet."

Red turned in the slop underneath us. I cracked her code from the back. Her pretty ass slapped against my thighs, and I gripped her meaty cheeks in my hands. I could barely hold on. She was moving too fast. With her cheeks being so slippery, I had to let go. This time, I watched the rain pounce on her back while I tackled her on my knees. Mud splashed all over us, and after a while, we said to hell with it. We rolled in that shit, with her eventually on top, giving me a ride I could force to the back of my mind, but wouldn't be able to forget. I didn't know how either of us would drive home, but we managed to put on our clothes and jet as is. By the time we made it to her crib, the mud had dried on our skin, making it real stiff. We cleaned up in the shower, but fucked again before shutting it down for the night. Red was sound asleep, but I lay wide awake puffing on a cigar and staring at an annoying-ass ceiling fan that was squeaking. I turned to look at her, and minutes later, I got my clothes out of the dryer and left. I hitched a ride with a black man going in my direction to pick up my car.

RED

What a night! I didn't know if I had been dreaming or not, especially when I woke up and saw that Bones had left. I could still smell a hint of his masculine cologne, though, and my coochie was real tender from the shit he spun on me. He didn't even have to do a bitch like that. Damn!

At first, I was so afraid that he would crack my face again. After flipping me that quarter, I was done. Then, Nate came in the back where I was and coaxed me to hang in there. Said that it would pay off for me. He damn sure was right about that. The money that he'd given me was right on time. However, what Bones delivered made this little plan so worth it.

But, unfortunately for me, I was starting to catch feelings for this nigga. I liked his ass, for real. I was concerned about my feelings getting in the way. I just didn't see where I could ever try to drug him, and then feel good about it. Behind all that hardness, he seemed . . . nice. He came off as someone who was hurt before and was very cautious of the females he fucked with. I was lucky to have gotten this far with him. I hoped to get even further. At this point, I wasn't so sure if Nate would come out on the losing end or not. I was seriously considering taking the money and running.

By eight o'clock in the morning, Nate was already ringing my phone and texting me. I was in the tub, relaxing with a whole lot of bubbles surrounding me and thinking about my muddy fuck session with Bones. That was some wild and crazy shit. I didn't think he would participate, but I suspected that I would have to try something out of the norm in order for him to make a move.

I answered my cell phone and listened to Nate yell at me about not answering sooner.

"My name ain't Alexis, so calm the fuck down," I said. "I just woke up, and I needed to take a hot bath before I did anything else."

"Why's that? Did you fuck him last night? Or did you allow that other stripper to do it?"

"She didn't have anything coming, and we both know that she's not his type. For the record, I did fuck him last night. He just left my place this morning."

I gave Nate explicit details. I could tell he was jealous. I didn't get why he secretly despised Bones so much, but if I asked, I was sure he wouldn't tell me.

"I don't believe you. Bones wouldn't do no shit like that, so stop living in a fantasy world. He's too private. The thought of anybody seeing y'all would've been on his mind."

"I have no reason to lie to you. If you'd like to come over here and measure the increase in the size of my pussy, feel free. I'm thoroughly enjoying myself with him, and believe me when I say we didn't care if anyone was watching us. Besides, we were next to the building where very few people can park. I made sure of that."

Nate was quiet, which meant he was pondering and scheming some more. I didn't know why he felt as if he could trust me. There was a chance that I would make this shit backfire on him.

"Did he tell you his real name yet?"

"Nope."

"Did he kiss you yet?"

"Nope. We came real close, but not yet."

"Then he ain't feeling you like he needs to be feeling you. Don't keep throwing the pussy at him all the time. Do something special for the nigga. Tap into his heart and make him believe that you really care about him. You know how y'all bitches do it."

I clicked the end button to disconnect my call with him. He irked the fuck out of me. How dare he ask for a favor, and then think it was okay to keep dissing me. I guess he didn't realize that I had the balls, yes, Bones's balls, in my court.

Nate called back, and after the third time, I answered. "What do you want?"

"I want you to listen up and stop tripping off shit I say to you. Bones will be shooting hoops today at the Civic Center. Did he give you his number yet?"

"Nope."

"Bye, bitch. I'ma get somebody else on this nigga 'cause the only thing yo' ass interested in is laying on yo' back."

"You can do whatever you wish, but remember this. I have the majority of your money in my pocket. If you want it to go to waste, fine, go find somebody else to do your dirty work. There will be no hard feelings, because with or without your money, Bones and me still gon' be hooking up."

This time, Nate hung up on me. I wasn't sure what his next move would be, but I was sure that I was going to stop by the Civic Center to see Mr. Bones.

Since it was Sunday, I didn't feel like working. I wasn't sure what time Bones would be at the Civic Center, but by three o'clock in the afternoon, I was dressed to impress in a yellow stretch minidress that went well with my cocoa skin. I sported gold accessories and a black and gold belt was around my waist. My natural hair sat high on my head and had been sprayed with a little sheen. I glistened my lips with nude gloss, dolled up my lashes with thick mascara, then slipped into my boots. I definitely had style, and before I walked out of the door, I grabbed my short leather jacket.

I didn't know how long Bones had been at the Civic Center, but just as Nate had said, his car was parked outside with a few other cars. I was kind of nervous about going inside, but I already had my lie together, just in case he questioned me.

I walked into the Civic Center and saw a few kids swimming in an Olympic-sized pool to my left. To the right, I could hear a basketball thumping hard on the floor and several masculine voices sounded off. I went to the doorway to look inside and instantly became breathless. Bones had on a pair on hanging B-ball shorts and a black wife beater. The tats all over his arms and across his back made him look sexy as hell. His waves were lined to perfection, and his facial hair was trimmed well. I loved the narrowness of his serious eyes, and as I watched him play ball with two other dudes, I found myself in a trance. I could see his bulge through his shorts, and when he removed his wife beater to wipe his sweat, I wanted to crawl to that nigga and praise his good looks. If Nate thought I was going to help him do away with all this fineness, he was sadly mistaken. Fuck that shit. . . . The deal was definitely off!

I had been standing there for almost thirty minutes before Bones ever saw me. When he did, he tossed a chest pass to his nerdy friend that I'd seen him with quite often. His brows arched inward, and he wiped across his lips before coming my way. I walked further into the large gym and stood by several bleachers.

"What's up?" he said in a nasty tone. "How you know I was here? Are you following me or something?"

"No, I'm not. I stopped by your house to see if you wanted to check out a movie with me. Your grandmother told me you were here. Since I was still in the neighborhood, I stopped by to holla."

"Bones," his friend yelled, "are you gon' finish the game or not?"

He turned around and held up his finger. "Give me a minute. I'm coming." He looked at me. "You didn't stop by my house, and my grandmother didn't tell you shit. When I'm done playing, I want the truth."

He jogged away to resume his game. I sat on the bleachers admiring the heck out of him and thinking hard about another lie I could tell him. Then again, why not just tell him the truth?

Bones was in no rush to get at me. He played several more games and didn't finish for at least another hour or so. I could've left, but bored I was not. I enjoyed seeing him hoop. He'd definitely missed his calling as a NBA player. He wasn't as tall as many of them, but he damn sure had some moves. He slapped hands with his friends and the nerdy one saluted him on his way out. He also spoke to me.

"I'm Theo," he said, shaking my hand. "Be easy on my boy, all right?"

I laughed and watched as Theo walked away. Bones and another older man headed my way.

"Is this you?" the older man said to Bones, referring to me.

"Naw, she's just a friend. But then again, maybe after tonight, she won't be."

I playfully rolled my eyes and blew off his comment. The older man advised us to have a safe evening and left. Bones tossed his wife beater over his shoulder. He stood in front of me, cracking his knuckles.

"Are you ready to tell me why you're here and how you knew I was here too?"

"I will tell you, only if you agree to go to the movies with me. I'll tell you while we're in my car."

Bones walked around me and headed toward the exit. I followed behind him, even though he was moving fast.

"A'ight," I said. "Slow down and wait."

He didn't stop until he reached his car. He leaned against the door with his arms crossed, muscles bulging. "Thirty seconds, then I'm out. Go."

My eyes shifted to the ground, then back to him. I released a deep sigh, then spoke. "I—"

He opened the door and got inside of his car. "You took too long. Gotta go."

Before I could say anything, he closed the door and sped off. I didn't know if I should've been mad or laughed at his actions. This nigga was a trip. I figured he was heading home to shower and change clothes. And when I drove off the parking lot, he appeared to be driving in the direction of his house. He knew I was behind him, but then we got stuck in traffic because the police had several streets blocked. Numerous people were standing around. I lowered my window to ask a lady on the corner what had happened. She informed me that a teenager had gotten shot. I shook my head, said a silent prayer, and waited for about thirty minutes until the police directed several cars in another direction. By then, Bones had beat me to his house. When I got there, he was standing on the porch tying his tennis shoes. His head shot up; then he cocked his neck from side to side. He smooth walked his way to my car, presenting so much swag. He bent over to look inside the window.

"I can already tell that you gon' be a pain in my ass."

"And I can tell that you really like me, but you prefer to be an asshole. Now, please get in the car so I can finish what I was about to say."

"What you say don't matter. You already admitted to being a liar, and now I won't believe anything you say."

"That's fine and dandy. So with that being said, will you please get in the car?"

"I don't like to see women begging, so—"

Bones opened the door and got inside. I could see his grandmother peeking out the window. When she saw me looking at her, she opened the curtains wider. I started to mention it to Bones, but I kept her overprotectiveness to myself.

As I drove off, he lowered the visor to look in the mirror. While brushing his waves, I started to answer his question from earlier.

"I drove by your house earlier and didn't see your car. I didn't stop, but to my surprise, I saw your car parked on the Civic Center's parking lot. I started to keep it moving, but then I wanted to see you again. Been thinking a lot—too much about you—so I went inside to see what was up. That there is the truth."

Bones flipped up the visor, and then put his brush back in his pocket. He looked over at me, didn't dare smile. "Bullshit. Next question. Where are you taking me?"

"How you gon' call me a liar and—"

He reached over and placed his hand over my mouth. "Let it go. Where are you taking me?"

He removed his hand. I changed the subject by answering his question. "I would like to go to the movies. But you over there acting like you really don't want to be here. Why are you so cold like that, and must you always be so serious? I mean, damn. I have barely seen you smile."

"What movie?"

He was cut and dry. I just shook my head before pulling the car over to the curb. "Okay, let's settle this shit, once and for all," I said. "Are you feeling me or not? Am

I wasting my time, or is it okay for us to kick it every now and then? I'm not trying to be your girlfriend or anything like that, but I prefer to hang with niggas who want to have some fun."

Bones sat silently for a few seconds, then spoke up. "Let's go have what you consider fun then."

"But you didn't answer my questions. And if we're going to have some fun, I need to know your real name. Mine is Renita, but please continue to call me Red."

"Renita," he said, stroking the hair on his chin. "Interesting."

"What's so damn interesting about it?"

"It's interesting that Bones is going to the movies with Renita. I suggest that you hurry up and make a move, if you don't want to be late."

"I will, if and when you answer my questions and tell me your name."

Bones's eyes narrowed as he gazed straight-ahead while licking his bottom lip. He was bothered. Thinking. Plotting. And irritated. I didn't give a fuck. He cleared his throat, then turned his head in my direction.

"I'm not gon' tell you my real name, and I'm never interested in women like you. So, to sum it all up, and just so you know what direction I'm coming from, I don't have to show interest in the people I fuck. You and I, all we do is fuck. Sex is simply sex. Don't expect more. I'm not the one to catch feelings over a piece of good-ass pussy. And I hope great dick don't twist things in yo' head."

My mouth dropped wide open. I guess this muthafucka told me, huh? I mean, stop playing the piano, close all of the windows and doors, and let's get the fuck out. His ass was too right to the point for me, but at least he was honest. The last thing I wanted him to know was that his words had a big bite. No, let me rephrase that. They stung like hell. But if he thought I was going to be salty about the shit, he had me all fucked up. Like always when I got dissed by niggas, I put on my happy face and kept it moving. I did, however, have to clear something up with this nigga, just in case he thought he'd put me in check.

"Before I drive off and we go to the movies, let me make one thing you said clear. The term 'women like you' could possibly mean you're referring to my profession, right? Let me just say that you have no idea where I come from, and you don't know why I must do what I do. Life probably dealt you a shitty hand, just like me, so don't you dare sit there and attempt to judge me for making tough decisions to better myself. You haven't a clue how much courage it takes to be a stripper and pretend that every fucking thing around me is all good. I put up with hella shit from niggas, and instead of walking around, like you, with a goddamn frown on my face all day, I bite my tongue and deal with the choices I made. You may not like them, but here's the truth and only the truth. I don't give a fuck, and I'ma keep on smiling each and every time niggas like you think it's okay to belittle me and make me feel as if I'm not good enough. Maybe not for Mr. Bones, but definitely for someone else more deserving."

I guess I told him. It was his turn to take the mic. To no surprise, he shrugged and pointed straight-ahead. "The movie theater is that way. Are we going or not?"

Don't ask me why I drove to the movies with this nigga, but I did. I kept quiet, though, and didn't have much else to say. The only time I spoke was when we stood in line, debating what to go see.

"I don't care what we watch," he said. "This is yo' bill, not mine."

Since I offered to take him to the movies, I didn't mind paying. But he could at least pay for the popcorn and sodas. We stood in line to get some, and when the cashier told us the amount, Bones stood with his hands in his pockets. I paid for those items too, but in the end, the money Nate was going to give me would pay for everything. I was now considering executing the plan to put this fool to sleep.

I chose a boring, stupid-ass movie on purpose. I had hoped that no one else would join us in the theater, but as soon as the previews got started, two white couples came in. Bones and I sat in the far back. Nigga chomped on my popcorn as if he'd bought it. I removed my jacket, sipped from my soda, and scrolled through Facebook to see what was up.

"What's this movie about?" he asked.

"I honestly do not know, but I heard it was good."

Bones passed me the popcorn, and then slumped down in his seat. We both had attitudes, and even though I said I wouldn't let what he'd said get underneath my skin, I did.

The movie got started, and we hadn't said two words to each other. I was bored out of my mind, and I kept hearing him release deep sighs. The actors in the movie were horrible, and the comedy they presented was so fucking corny. Maybe I should've opted for an action/comedy movie with Kevin Hart in it. Since I hadn't, and this movie was so bad, I intended to ask for a refund when we left.

I scrolled through my Facebook page again, reading the comments and looking at pictures. That kept me busy . . . until Bones took the phone from my hand. He put it in his pocket, then lifted me up from my seat, and sat me on his lap. His hands massaged my legs, and when he inched over to my inner thighs, I closed them. After spewing his harsh words, I was in no mood to let this happen. But the feel of his hard dick pressing against my ass made me excited. His hand moved closer to my goodies, and as he slipped his finger inside of my silk thong, my legs fell apart. My mini stretched upward, and Bones lifted it to my waist. While putting on a condom, he rubbed his thick fingers along my hairless slit, making it moister by the second. The crotch section of my thong was soaking wet, but in an effort to get at me like he wanted to, he ripped my thong away from my skin. He lifted me to receive his dick and pushed one of his fingers into me at the same time. His thumb, however, turned speedy circles around my swollen clit. I wanted to scream, shout, holler . . . make some kind of noise, but I didn't want the people way in front of us to turn around. Instead, I muffled my lips and grinded hard to satisfy the tingling feeling between my legs that was increasing by the minute.

I was on-fucking-fire. His heavy breathing implied that something had been stirring up inside of him too. When he pulled down the top half of my mini, exposing my breasts, I slightly turned on his lap. He lowered his head, and I offered him a chunky portion of my right breast. His teeth lightly bit at my nipple, his thumb circled around my clit, his finger fucked me so well, and his dick was coated with my heavy cream.

Things got even better when he stood and bent me over the plush seat in front of us. With all of this man . . . a real man behind me displaying sexiness, braveness, strength, and creativeness, my heart pounded fast. A sticky mess was building between my legs, and they were straddled wide open as Bones hit that shit like he was digging for precious gold. He held on tight to my hips. My eyes fluttered, and I released soft moans that helped to relieve some of what I was feeling. I hadn't a clue how I was going to silence my orgasm, and sure enough, when it came, Bones reached around to my mouth, covering it with his hand.

Luckily for me, there was finally some action happening on the big screen. The volume was extremely loud.

My body went limp, and I fell back on the seat with Bones. As a nice gesture, he used my thong to wipe the juices dripping from my pussy. He then straightened my minidress and held my waist as he placed me back in my seat to the left of him. I saw him remove the condom and drop it into the empty bucket of popcorn. After that, he relaxed back in the seat and stared ahead to watch the movie.

"Still bored?" he questioned.

I didn't hesitate to answer. "Yes. A little."

"So am I. Take me home."

Without saying another word, I got up and drove him back to his house. There was pure silence in the car, and before he made his exit, he spun around to face me.

"The next time you come see me, I want to have some of that so-called fun you mentioned. The direction you trying to move us in, I ain't feeling it."

"And what direction is that?"

"I'll say this," he said, then opened the door. "You know better than I do."

He got out of the car and shut the door. I couldn't help but wonder if he knew what Nate and I had been up to. It was definitely time for me to wipe my hands clean. Something warned me inside that Bones wasn't the kind of nigga to fuck with. In addition to that, the tables were starting to turn on me. I was falling for him, instead of him falling for me.

BONES

I was on my fourth mission for Mango. He had been lining my pockets with a whole lot of paper. The nigga was more down-to-earth than I thought he would be, and over the past few weeks, I had already earned his respect. I handled my business, brought him back souvenirs, and collected my money. He shared a lot of information with me about the streets, the drug game, and spoke about many of the key players. He also mentioned shady niggas who were trying to get over on him. I was disappointed to hear him mention Nate and Theo's names. He referred to them as snakes and encouraged me to watch my back. While I already had some feelings about our friendship not being as tight as it had been before, I stressed to Mango that day that there was nothing or no one who would ever come between me and my boys.

"I used to feel the same way about my boys too," he said. "But money changes people. And the more you make, niggas start to hate. They start to plot against you. I don't give a damn how long they've been in yo' corner. These bitches out here are snakes too. You definitely have to keep yo' eyes on them. They will use that hot oven to fuck wit' yo' head and suck you right in. Befo'e you know it, you'll get burnt and be all fucked up. I'm just telling you this straight from an old nigga who knows something. You're one of the brightest, most intelligent, and skillful niggas I know. It would trouble me to see you go up, then fall down."

I listened and nodded, nodded and listened. Sometimes, it was best not to say anything. Just sit back and take it all in. He really couldn't tell me much about Theo or Nate that I didn't already know. And his advice about women wasn't really an eye-opener either. I knew all about the power of pussy. That was one of the reasons why Red would always be on the outside trying to get in. My instincts said she was trouble. I could feel it, each and every time we were together. There was something about her that gave me bad vibes. Then there was something about her that I kind of liked. I loved her natural beauty. I appreciated how real she was in the car with me that day. I suspected that my harsh words would pull something like that out of her. It was obvious that she had her struggles too. We all coped in different ways. But unless those vibes went away when I was around her, all she would ever be to me was a sex partner with no benefits.

The last time I'd seen Red, or permitted her to see me, was over three weeks ago. Sometime last week, she unexpectedly stopped by my crib. I went to the door, told her I was entertaining company, and demanded that she not pay me any further pop-up visits. After that, I hadn't heard from her. I avoided going to the strip club, because I didn't want to see her.

Like all of the others, that nigga Skittles didn't see me coming. He was caught completely off guard by my staggering blow that crushed the middle of his face. He had just left his bitch's apartment, and I'd caught up with him on the parking lot. While standing in the middle of the street, he wobbled. Was dazed. His nose was busted, most likely broken. Blood poured over his lips and dripped from his chin. I waited for that fool to drop to the ground, but before he did, somebody clocked me in the back of my head with something real hard. This time, I was the one dazed. Slightly. I tried to shake that shit off, but then I was smashed in the head again.

"Who in the hell are you?" the woman shouted, before striking me again. "Don't you dare punch my damn man in the face, you idiot!"

This bitch had hit me in the head with the pointed heel of her fucking shoe. It hurt like hell. I touched the back of my head, and when I looked at my fingers, I saw blood. Not much, but enough to make me want to beat her ass. I didn't know who to pivot to first. Finish off Skittles or deal with his woman who was in a rage. I seriously thought I could handle him first, but as I shook my head, again, to shake off the blows from her shoe, she kept charging me. She hopped on my back and started pounding on my head like she was holding a hammer. I flipped the bitch backward, causing her to hit the ground. Hard. That still didn't stop her. She charged at me again. This time, her face was met with my knuckles. I hated to go there with any woman, but this trick was throwing punches at me like she was Floyd "Money" Mayweather.

"Come on, nigga," she said, still swinging her fists. "Is that all you got?"

By now, Skittles's ol' punk ass had broke out running. I damn sure didn't want him to get away, especially since Mango had already given me half of the money to take care of him. I hurried to settle my differences with his woman. In a matter of seconds, I tripped her to the ground and grabbed one of her legs. I hurried to look between them, making sure I saw a pussy, not a dick, because she seemed too strong. The pussy was definitely there, but in order to stop her in her tracks, I used much force to snap her ankle to the right, and then back to the left. It cracked and dangled in my hand. Hearing her shriek and whimper out loudly didn't bother me one bit. I had a bigger fish to fry.

Skittles had already hopped into his car, and trying to catch him, I ran fast to the only exit of the parking lot. I figured that he would try to run me over, and sure enough, he did. I heard the engine revving up, but as soon as he slammed on the accelerator, I dove for a big-ass brick that was in my sights and pitched it through the windshield. Glass shattered and scattered everywhere. The car jumped the curb and smashed into a streetlight. The horn sounded off while Skittles crawled out of the car with a deep gash on the left side of his forehead. He staggered forward with a 9 mm in his hand. It was cocked sideways and aimed at my head.

"You's a dead nigga," he said, limping my way. His bitch was in the background yelling foul shit and screaming too. Several people had come outside to see what in the fuck was going on. Sirens could be heard from afar. I wasn't sure if I was going to catch a bullet in my front or in my back. What I figured was, I'd better get the fuck out of there, fast. Without going to my car, instead, I dashed across the street. I could hear the sound of bullets spraying the path behind me. I hurdled over some bushes and felt one of the bullets graze the side of my hand. I shook off the pain and flew through a side street that was my outlet to leaving the chaos erupting behind me in the wind. I was completely out of breath, and by the time I'd made it home, it was almost an hour and a half later. I hurried inside, locking the door behind me. As soon as I turned around, my grandmother stood near the kitchen's doorway with her arms folded.

"What's going on?" she said, looking at the dripping blood from my hand.

"Nothing. I hurt my hand, climbing over a fence."

"Don't lie to me, Bones. I can always tell when you lying, and I hope and pray that you ain't out there doin' nothin' that you ain't got no business doin'. Those streets ain't nothin' to play with out there, and innocent people and children are gettin' killed every day."

I wasn't in the mood for one of my grandmother's lectures. And instead of listening to her, I made a move to the bathroom and closed the door. I turned on the faucet and ran water over my hand. The graze wasn't as bad as I thought it was, but I had lost enough blood. I kept applying pressure. The blood started to slow down, so I poured peroxide over my hand, then wrapped it with gauze. I played doctor on the back of my head too, and if I ever saw that bitch again who hit me with that shoe, she would pay for making me bleed. My whole body was aching, so I popped four aspirin in my mouth, then left the bathroom. Yet again, my grandmother was waiting to lecture me.

"You'd better be careful, Bones. Let me see yo' hand," she said.

"No." I walked around her and headed toward my room. She followed behind me.

"Hang on to yo' secrets, but don't you ever bring any of that mess into my home. If you's out there doin' somethin' you ain't got no business doin', then I'ma have to ask you to leave here. I'm too old for this shit. You know good and doggone well that I'm too old to be worryin' about you."

I stood in the doorway and released a deep sigh. "You don't have to worry about me. I promise you that I'm not out there doing anything wrong. I didn't want to show you my hand because I already wrapped it. But once I take this off, I'll show it to you then. Now, can I please get some rest? I worked overtime today. I'm tired."

My grandmother didn't reply. The look on her face implied that she didn't believe me. She was too smart to believe the hype, and I knew it.

I kissed her cheek, then closed my bedroom door. After I plopped down on the bed, I reached for my phone to call

Mango. I told him everything that had happened. Was surprised by his concern for my well-being.

"You did the right thang by gettin' the fuck out of there. That nigga probably wondering why you were trying to get after him. At this point, though, I recommend that you take him out. Leaving that kind of shit behind can get messy in the long run. It's up to you. Whatever you decide, I'm down with it and I got yo' back."

Mango said he'd send somebody over to the apartment complex to get my car. And within the hour, it was parked in front of my house with the keys in the ignition. I wanted to holla at Nate and Theo about what had been going down, but then again, I was glad that they didn't know shit. They had inquired about the extra paper they'd seen me with, but I told them that I'd been doing several more floor stripping and waxing gigs that paid good money. I'd told my grandmother the same thing, but with her, I knew the only person I had been fooling was myself. It was just a matter of time when she caught on to my new profession, provided to me by a black man who would ultimately, one day, make me very wealthy.

RED

Nate and I stood in one of the back rooms at the strip club arguing. I had given some of his money back to him and told him to keep me out of whatever he had planned for Bones. Nate was mad as hell at me. He backed me into a corner, where he caged me in and wouldn't let me go.

"If you touch me," I warned, "I swear I'ma have security up in here so fast, wearing yo' ass out. Now back the fuck up, Nate. You not gon' get me to change my mind, and whether you want to believe me or not, I have made little or no progress with him. He ain't biting. That's why I'm done fucking with you and your *friend*."

"I doubt that shit, and if he ain't biting, he damn sure still sucking. You done caught some feelings for that nigga. Now you want out. It don't work like that, Red. You should already know that niggas like me don't play games where you can come and go as you please."

I pursed my lips and pushed Nate back. He reached out and slapped the shit out of me. "Don't put yo' fucking hands on me, ho! I will kill you and paint this goddamn room with your blood! Security won't be able to save you, and neither will that nigga Bones. Now, I'ma need you to finish what you started. If you don't, you will definitely pay the price!"

I held the side of my sore face, rubbing it. My eyes stayed locked with Nate's. I didn't care if he hit me again, and I continued to stand by my words.

"Nigga, get out the paintbrush and start painting then. I will never do anything else that you demand of me, and I'm going to tell Bones everything about you. You are a goddamn animal, Nate. Bones deserves much more than a backstabbing, dirty-ass friend like you!"

I gathered spit in my mouth and sprayed it right in his face. I already suspected that I would catch a beat down from his ass tonight, and the least I could do was get in a few licks myself. But right after the spitting incident, Nate picked me up and slammed me on a table. He grabbed me by my collar, and then threw me across the room. I fell hard on my knees, and before I could get up, he backhanded me across the face.

"I bet yo' ass won't be pretty no mo'," he said.

I looked into the devil's eyes, knowing that Nate wanted to kill me. But after he punched me in my stomach and bit down hard on my lips, somebody knocked on the door.

He paused his hand in midair. "Who is it?" he yelled. "We're busy!"

"Unlock the door," Stoney said. He was the owner of the club, and he must've heard all of the ruckus that was going on inside. "Now, Nate! Open it!"

I held my hand over my bloody mouth. Couldn't believe that nigga had bit me on my lips, and my stomach was so sore that I had to comfort it too. Nate shot me a dirty look, and then he unlocked the door. Stoney came inside with a frown washed across his face. He looked at me, then at Nate whom he was very cool with.

"Nigga, you can't be doing this kind of shit to my girls. You fucking up my money, and this right here is my main prize. Whatever beef you got with her, it needs to be squashed. I need her to get out there and do her thing tonight. Too many muthafuckas waiting on her. How in the hell am I gon' send her out there looking like that?"

Nate frowned too. He cut his eyes at Stoney, then looked at me. "Go clean yourself up, bitch. You hoes be getting real lucky. One of these days, there will be nobody around to save y'all."

With tears in my eyes, I ran past Nate and Stoney. The last thing I felt like doing tonight was stripping, but when I stepped outside of the door, I heard a few niggas chanting my name. I went into the dressing room and looked at myself in the mirror. My face was fucked up, but it wasn't anything a bunch of makeup couldn't hide. I wiped my tears knowing that no matter what had happened, the show must go on.

BONES

I didn't feel like hanging with the fellas tonight, but when Theo called and begged me to meet him and Nate at the club, I changed my mind. I hadn't hung out with them in a minute. Kind of got tired of hanging around the house and hearing my grandmother complain about something not being right. She was knocked out when I left, and before I made my appearance at the club, I decided to go handle some unfinished business.

Mango said that it was my decision to ultimately decide how to handle Skittles. The truth was, I didn't like how things had gone down. I was sure that nigga would remember me if he saw me again, and his bitch would too.

In knowing so, I did another quick drive-by. This time, I chilled outside until I saw his girlfriend's car swerve into a parking spot. She got out of the car on crutches, and he helped her to the door. They went inside of their apartment, and after twenty minutes or so, the lights went out. I sat smoking a blunt while also kicking back a fifth of Hennessy. Once it was all gone, I picked up the 9 milli next to me and screwed on the silencer. I got out of the car, carefully watching my surroundings as I made my way to the front door. I turned the knob. It was locked. There was a patio with a sliding door on the side, so I checked to see if it provided easy access. Locked too. Still, it was easy for me to slide a card inside and wiggle the inside handle. Once it clicked, the door slid right over. Soft music hummed throughout the raggedy-ass apartment, and I could hear his girlfriend yelling out for him to "travel deep inside." I waited before interrupting their sex session, and the second I heard Skittles talk his shit, I suspected that he had busted a nut. At least I had enough consideration to let the man get off . . . before killing him. I pushed on the door—Boldly marched inside with no fear whatsoever. With his girlfriend's legs still poured over his shoulders, and his back facing me, I pulled the trigger, twice. The gun jerked. Sent two speeding bullets whistling through the air and into his back. A gargling sound came from his mouth, and then he fell forward. A loud scream erupted from his girlfriend's mouth. I walked slowly and casually over to the bed . . . eased the gun into her mouth, and pressed my finger against my lips. "Shhhh," I warned.

Tears poured down her face. She shook her head, implying no. I stared into her fearful eyes and nodded. "Yes," I said in a whisper. "Don't take it personal."

I pulled the trigger and quickly turned away. As I walked to my car, I couldn't help but to think about the kind of man I was becoming.

For whatever reason, the club seemed more thick than usual. Several birthday celebrations were going on, and the table we normally sat at was packed with more niggas. Theo waved for me to come have a seat. I spotted Nate at the bar getting some drinks.

"You are always late," Theo said. "Man, we hit the jackpot last night. Got into this banker's 6.7 million-dollar crib and racked up! You need to stop by Nate's crib tomorrow to see all the shit we got. Some of that jewelry may cost a fortune, but you know we gots to be careful about how we unload that shit."

"Real careful. I'll definitely stop by tomorrow to check out things."

Theo gave me dap. I chilled next to him to holla about what had been going down with my supposedly-new-gig at the church. When Nate came to the table, his face was scrunched. I could tell he was on edge about something. I looked at his knuckles; saw bruises and a few scratches. I figured that he and Alexis must've been at it again. In an effort not to make him more miserable, I brought up the past. Started talking shit about elementary and high school that made him laugh.

"You were the one who had a crush on that ugly-ass teacher," Nate said, referring to our English teacher, Mrs. Bell. "She had a fat ass, though. And you know yo' ass lied when you said you fucked her. You got in trouble for that shit."

I pointed to Theo. "Uh . . . wasn't me. Theo was the one who started that rumor, but I was the one who got suspended. I did have a crush on her, though. But have y'all seen that bitch lately? Man, I saw her ass at the grocery store. Damn near wanted to cry! She looked like an alien."

We all laughed. Nate continued to stress how ugly she was from the get-go. I disagreed. We debated another issue that had happened in junior high school, and as several strippers stopped by to direct our attention elsewhere, we dropped a few dollars and continued to talk about the good old times. But when Red came by, she kind of kept her distance. Nate cut his eyes at her a few times, and I saw him wince too. Red never did come my way, but as I looked at her face, I could tell something was wrong. Her lips looked swollen and for her to never wear a lot of makeup, tonight, she had on plenty. As I stared at her, I could see Nate staring at me. I shifted my eyes in his direction. He turned his head and started a conversation with Jerry who sat next to him, but his actions were too late. I assumed that Nate had beat Red's ass. Question is . . . why?

After nearly everyone was gone, including my boys, I waited in my car for Red. This time, she walked out with two other strippers, and while they laughed, Red had a sad look on her face. That was rare. I got out of my car and called her name. She slowly walked my way.

"What's up?" she said, shooting me a fake smile. "I thought you had left."

"Nah." I nudged my head toward my car. "Get inside. Let's talk."

She got inside, crossing one blemish-free leg over the other. "What's on your mind, or should I be asking, what kind of position would you rather see me in tonight? The only time you ever come around is when you're hungry for some pussy. I take it that day and time has arrived."

I ignored her comment and didn't beat around the bush. "What happened to your face?"

Her brows rose. "My face? What do you mean by that?"

"You know what the fuck I mean, so stop playing games. Who hit you?"

She sat silent for a few seconds, then crossed her arms. "Why, Bones? It's not like you care anyway. You've made that quite obvious, so why does it matter?"

"Because it does. Tell me who hit you."

"I'll tell you, if you let me do one thing."

I shook my head, displaying my frustrations with her. "Here we go with this shit again. Believe it or not, I'm not here to—"

Red leaned closer, trying to kiss me. I backed away and put my hand in front of her swollen lips. She remained very close while searching my eyes. "A kiss, Bones. All I want is one simple kiss, and you won't even give me that. I'll tell you who did this to me, if you give me a kiss."

"No deal. And for the record, this is the last time I'm gon' ask you about who did this to you. Now is your chance to tell me the truth. If you don't, I never want to see you again."

Red backed away from me and remained silent for a while. She fidgeted with her hands, and then took a hard swallow. "Stoney did it. You know he owns this place, and he was mad at me for not showing up for two days last week. He lost money, and when I tried to tell him why I was absent, he still hit me. I spit on his ass, and he went crazy. He later apologized, but between us, I'll be looking for another place to work real soon."

"That's your story, and you're sticking to it?"

Red looked me straight in the eyes and nodded. "Believe it or not, that's the truth. Now, getting back to the kiss you owe me."

"You'll get it one day, just not today. Now, gon' and get out of here. Take your sweet self home and doctor up that pretty face of yours." I cracked a tiny smile that almost knocked Red out of her seat. She looked shocked.

"Oh my God," she said. "You have teeth. They are actually there, and I barely get to see them because you never smile."

"You may not have seen them, but you have definitely felt them biting on your nipples, haven't you?"

"Of course. And if you have any desire to bite on them tonight, Mr. Vampire, all you have to do is say the word."

"What's the word?"

"Open, please."

"That's two words."

"And?"

"And if you open, I wouldn't mind driving right in."

Red reached for the handle and opened the door. "Yeah, that's what I thought. You may have some people fooled, Mr. Bones, but not me. Follow me. And this time when I wake up in the morning, yo' ass better still be there."

She got out of the car, and I followed her home. For the majority of the night, we stayed up talking and playing cards. She seemed to be . . . sweet. I couldn't deny that I was starting to like her a little bit more. I sat her on my lap, and we didn't indulge ourselves into a heated sex session until four o'clock in the morning.

As soon as she fell asleep, I put my clothes on and jetted.

I stood outside talking to Mango as he walked around with his German shepherd, Prince. He praised me for what I'd done to Skittles, but was mad as hell because Skittles had a healthy stash of his money somewhere and nobody knew where it was. Three of Mango's partners were sent to trash Skittles's apartment to look for the money. They came up empty, but told Mango how pretty the scene was after I'd done my damage. Mango was so satisfied with what I'd done that he lined my pockets with more paper. He asked me to check around about his money and let him know if I hear anything. His dog stopped to take a dump, and that's when Mango reached into his pocket and handed me another three-by-five picture.

"That's yo' next mission," he said. "I don't have to tell you who that nigga is."

I looked at the picture. My face fell flat. It was a picture of Theo with sneaky eyes and looking nerdy as fuck with his glasses on. I quickly gave the picture back to Mango.

"That's one mission I can't accomplish. Sorry, man. You'll have to get somebody else to do your dirty work on that one. And being truthful, I will warn him that you're looking for him."

Mango sucked his teeth and swallowed hard. He called for one of his boys. "Take Prince inside," he said. "Bones and me need to have a serious talk."

The man grabbed Prince's leash and went inside. Mango started to slow walk with his hands in his pockets. I walked beside him.

"You're too smart to be a fool, Bones. I know Theo is yo' boy, but all he really is, is a flunky for Nate. Theo will turn his back on you in a heartbeat. Don't you ever thank that if he was in the same position as you, and I had given him yo' picture, that he would have given it back and refused to follow through."

"I know Theo well. He's good people. Following behind Nate or not, he would never betray me. Nate, however, is a different story. Something has been up with him, but I haven't rested my finger on it yet."

"One day you will. Until then, here's the truth. You can't trust nobody. Not even me. And the day you realize about what I'm saying to you, is the day I will help to make you one powerful man. You the kind of nigga who will one day go down in history around here. But the first thing you must do is wise up and recognize when fake muthafuckas are staring you right in the face."

"I hear what you saying, but tell me what it is that you know about Theo that I don't."

"Theo has been dodging me. He hasn't paid me any of my money in months. Normally, I give niggas thirty to sixty days to pay up. After that, I start looking for them. I question his loyalty to you because, when I inquired about yo' assistance before, he said you were a soft punk who hadn't grown up yet. Referred to you as a granny's boy and said you weren't man enough to handle thangs on yo' own. He also called you a wacko. Claimed you've been fucked up in the head ever since you watched yo' mama die in front of you. I could go on and on, but you know I ain't lying about the shit 'cause I never knew yo' mama was killed by her boyfriend."

I remained silent. Didn't know how to respond yet. The first thing I wanted to do was holla at Theo. While I assumed he probably said some of those things, I figured he didn't mean any harm. Maybe he was trying to make himself look good in Mango's eyes. Regardless, I stuck with my original decision.

"Out of all due respect, I won't reply to what you just said. But what I said before still stands. I hope this doesn't damage our business relationship, but that's for you to decide."

Mango stopped walking and reached for a handkerchief in his pocket. "You too good to them niggas, Bones. They don't deserve yo' friendship, but like many of us, you'll have to learn the hard way. Meanwhile, you and I will continue to do great things, and our business will, indeed, carry on."

He handed me another picture. I looked at it, then cracked my knuckles. "Now *this* one, I can handle."

Mango smiled. I didn't.

BONES

It took me less than two hours to find that nigga, Jesse J., who was in the picture. I broke his leg and had his whole fingernail in my pocket as a souvenir. I was on my way back to Mango's crib to collect the rest of my paper, but my plans changed when I got a call. I answered my cell phone, and Alexis was on the other end hollering and sobbing.

"I need you, please," she shouted. "Nate has hurt me for the last time! That nigga gon' die today if you don't do something about him. This time, he took my baby with him and left!"

I swallowed the oversized lump in my throat, then asked Alexis to calm down. "Ain't nobody gon' die, so stop saying that shit. Where is Nate now?"

"I don't know. He left here in a rage and took Brianna with him. I don't know if he's coming back or not, but if he does, this time, I'm going to kill him!"

I told Alexis I was on my way. Hopefully, Nate would be there by then, and we could talk this shit out. If anything, my intentions were to encourage them to go their separate ways and be done with it.

When I arrived at Nate's crib, the door was wide open. I walked inside and stepped over several pieces of broken furniture that had been strewn all over. My tennis shoes crunched on numerous pieces of glass on the floor, and it looked as if a tornado had blown through. Alexis sat on the couch in the living room, wiping her teary eyes with tissue. Her whole face looked swollen, and she had two black eyes. One was bloodshot red, and her bloody hands implied that she had been in a fight for her life. The TV had been kicked in, and when I saw Brianna's doll on the floor, I picked it up and placed it on the broken table. I stood in front of Alexis with a simple look washed across my face.

"It's no surprise what happened here, but what brought all of this about?" I questioned.

Alexis looked up at me, then shut her watery eyes. Several more tears flowed down her fucked-up face. "He knows, Bones. No more secrets because he's known what was up for a long time."

My stomach got tight. I eased on the couch next to her, staring straight-ahead. "How did he find out, and what did he say? Did you deny it?"

"He called me a bunch of bitches, hoes, sluts . . . every name he could possibly think of. I didn't deny anything. I admitted that you and I had slept together. He said that he got his info from Theo. Nate refused to believe him, but he said that he'd been paying attention, watching us. He could see how much I always wanted to be with you, and he feels as if you betrayed him in a major way. I don't know what he's going to do with Brianna, especially since I admitted to her not being his child."

"So, in other words, he knows that there is a possibility that she's mine."

Alexis caught an attitude with me. "She *is* yours! When you look at her, who do you see? Don't go talking that *possibility* shit, Bones. Especially when you already know the truth!"

My head swung in her direction. Anger crept on my face. "I don't know shit! All I know is what you told me, and I took your word for it! You still have not provided me with a blood test, so don't go talking that mess about what *I know* for a fact!"

"Blood test or no blood test, she looks like you!"

Alexis got up and stormed past me. I lowered my head, thinking about how, several years ago, I betrayed my friend. At that time, the power of pussy made me do some shit that I have forever regretted.

We were at a wild-ass swim party that day. Nearly everybody was drunk, and Nate's uncle's backyard was jammed with family, friends, and neighbors. Barbecue could be smelled from miles away, and to say that we were all having fun would be putting it mildly. I was there with my date, Jewel. She got so fucked up that I had to carry her upstairs to one of the bedrooms to sleep that shit off. I carefully laid her on the bed, and then closed the door behind me so that no one would disturb her.

As I tiptoed out of the room, Alexis stood near the steps waiting for me. She rocked a fire-red string bikini that barely covered the good stuff. Her silky long hair was parted through the middle and fell along the sides of her round face. Her sexiness couldn't be ignored, and at the time, I didn't have my head on straight. There were plenty of other sexy chicks at the party that night too, including my date who was now passed the fuck out. Nate had been by the pool looking at every piece of ass that passed by. He even ventured off earlier that night, and nobody knew where he was. Alexis, however, was pissed. And when she stood by the steps, I could see the hurt in her mysterious, yet seductive eyes.

"What's up with your friend?" she said. "Sometimes, he acts as if I'm not good enough for him. I know he cares for me, but has he always been like this?"

"Not always," I lied. Nate had always been a dog, but I wasn't going to tell her shit. Eventually, she'd learn all about his whorish ways.

"You're just taking up for him, because he's your friend."

I shrugged, then turned toward the bathroom. "I need to go take a leak. We can finish this conversation by the pool. That way, maybe Nate can explain himself."

Alexis laughed, and as she pivoted to go back down-stairs, I went into the bathroom. I had to piss so bad that I didn't bother to close the door. Just stood in relief with no shirt on and my dick hanging through the slit of my swim trunks. I scratched my head, and when I reached out to flush the toilet, that's when I saw Alexis standing near the doorway.

"Damn, Bones," she said. "I never would've suspected that you were holding down all of that."

I was shocked that she had been watching me, and the look in her eyes made me a little uncomfortable. "You should never assume anything," I said. "Especially when how much I'm holding ain't got nothing to do with you."

She came into the bathroom, closing the door behind her. I kept thinking that she was just fucking with me, and that Nate had sent her upstairs to do this because he knew I was intoxicated. Then again, this didn't seem like something Nate would do.

"I want you to feel something." Alexis strutted up to me and pressed her body against mine. I backed away, but stumbled just a little. She giggled, then reached for my hand, easing it into her bikini bottoms. Her pussy was soft. Fat. Smooth. So juicy that I was suddenly eager to slip my fingers into it. I pushed my index finger in as far as it would go, turning it inside of her. Her walls got wetter, and the gushing sounds of her fluids made me want to quickly substitute my finger for my dick.

"My pussy has never been this wet, Bones. And with a big dick like yours inside of it, there is no telling how much more you'll get out of me."

I damn sure wanted to know how much more. And at that moment, I didn't care that Alexis was Nate's girl. Hell, he'd had plenty of bitches, and all she seemed to be to him was just another pussy.

With that in mind, I sat on the toilet seat with Alexis's back facing me. She bent over, and her ass was too pretty and round for me not to taste it. Her pussy was too juicy not to be licked on, so I dipped my tongue into that shit too. She kept trying to move away from the deep sensation of my tongue, and when her pussy got too wet, I backed out of it and wiped my soaked mouth with my hand. I pulled her back to me and secured her waist while feeding her my inches.

"Ummmm, Boooones, that dick feels guuuud. You gon' make me want that muthafucka in my life forever."

At the time, I wanted her to want me and my dick. I gave her all of me, and as she quickly bounced up and down on me, her titties plopped out of her top. I massaged her breasts and slightly lifted myself from the toilet seat to dig all up in her. Right in the midst of us fucking each other's brains out, the door flew open. I snapped my head to the side. So did Alexis. There stood my boy, Theo, drunk and yelling that he had to piss. I stopped midstroke. Alexis, however, was in the process of having an orgasm, so she continued to grind hard on me.

"Damn!" Theo shouted, then laughed. "Uh, excuse the hell out of me for interrupting. Guess I'd better go seek another bathroom."

He shut the door so fast that I didn't get a chance to say anything. Alexis didn't seem to care that we'd been busted, but to cover my tracks, I had planned on telling Nate what had gone down. She begged me not to. Said he had already been kind of violent and she didn't want to upset him. And after the mind-blowing blow job she gave me, I couldn't say shit. I felt guilty as fuck.

Later that night, I shared with Theo how the shit got started. He even said that telling Nate wouldn't be a good idea. Said it was something that we should keep between us, but when Alexis announced that she was pregnant, and she and Nate had gotten closer, all I could do was hope and pray that the truth never came to light. Only three of us knew what was up, and I expected for the three of us to take that secret to our graves.

Thinking about Brianna, I jumped up from the couch. Whether she was mine or not, I didn't want Nate to do anything stupid. I walked toward the back and saw Alexis standing in their bedroom putting bullets into a gun.

"Who in the hell are you gon' use that on? Nate or me?"

"I already told you what I was going to do. Too bad if you don't believe me this time."

"Oh, I believe you. But I also know that Brianna wouldn't want you to do that. You gotta be around to take care of her, and niggas like Nate ain't worth you going to jail."

Alexis didn't respond. She slammed the dresser drawer shut, then tucked the gun behind her back. "Are you going to go find him, or shall I?"

"Let me go take care of this. I have an idea where he may be."

Alexis plopped on the bed and rubbed her forehead. She gazed at the floor, shaking her head. "Whatever you do, please bring my baby home." She turned in my direction, confirming what she had said before. "She is our child. Please bring her home to me."

Not saying a word, I calmly walked out.

I had never used Red's phone number, but I called it today. No answer. Suspecting that I would find Nate there, I drove to her place. To no surprise, his car was parked on the parking lot. I had a bad-ass feeling about how all of this was going to go down, but I was prepared. I wasted no time going to Red's door and knocking. It took her a few minutes to answer, but she opened the door with a grin on her face.

"Well, well, well," she said. "What brings you by? I guess you're hungry for me again, huh?"

I lightly pushed on the door and walked inside. "More than you know."

Red closed the door behind me. She wore a short silk robe, and as far as I could see, there was nothing underneath it. My eyes scanned every inch of her place that I could see.

"Where is he?" I said, sitting on the arm of the couch.

Her brows rose. "Where is who?"

"Nate."

She shrugged. "Uh, he's not here. Why would he be here?"

"Because you're fucking that nigga, that's why."

"I don't know where you're getting your info from, but no, I'm not fucking him."

Red was starting to upset me. This whole situation was already fucked up, and I hated a bitch to stand before me, smile in my fucking face, and lie.

"You full of shit."

I got up and started looking for that nigga myself. Red followed behind me as I knocked shit over and cleared everything that was in my path.

"What in the hell are you doing?" she hollered out. "I told you his ass wasn't here. Why are you over here trying to run shit?"

I ignored her and opened several of her closets. I pulled out clothes, blankets, shoes . . . everything that I could to see if Nate was somewhere hiding. Looked under the bed, couch, in the bathroom . . . even in the laundry room.

"I can't believe this shit!" Red yelled from behind me. "Have you lost your goddamn mind?"

I swiped my hand across all of the perfumes on her dresser, causing them to crash on the floor and break. "Where is he?" I yelled, then swung around to look at Red. The devious look in my eyes implied that she'd better come clean—quick. My heart raced and my hands were starting to curl into tight fists.

Red's eyes shifted to my hands, then back to my tight face. She blinked tears from her eyes and sucked in a deep breath. "He's not here, but he may be over at another chick's house who lives over here. I saw his car earlier—"

This bitch was seriously trying to play me like a fool. Before I knew it, I reached out and snatched her mutha-fucking neck so tight that her eyes looked as if they were about to pop from the sockets. My hand trembled as my grip got tighter and tighter. Red couldn't say a word. Tears seeped from the corners of her eyes, and she struggled to keep them open.

"Where is he?" I hollered through gritted teeth.

She slowly moved her head from side to side, gagging as she attempted to speak. I couldn't make out a word she'd said, and the only thing that caused me to loosen my grip was a hard knock on the door.

"Red!" Nate shouted. "Open the door!"

Thinking that maybe I had fucked up, I quickly released her neck. She immediately sucked in several deep breaths and covered her mouth as she coughed and gagged. Nate knocked a few more times. I pointed my finger at Red. "Do *not* move. Stay there."

She fell back on the bed, then curled herself up, still trying to catch her breath. I hurried to the front door. Nate got the shock of his life when he looked up and saw me standing there.

"Damn," he said with a leather jacket and jeans on. Hands in his pockets. "I didn't know you were here. I was over at ol' girl's place in apartment 310. She asked me to pick up a package from Red. She here?"

Maybe he had been in apartment 310, but I knew Nate had heard Red coughing. And I was also positive that the look on my face told him something wasn't right. He came inside, suspicions growing.

"Yeah, she's here, but my question to you is, where is Brianna? Before you say anything, I already know that you are aware of what went down between me and Alexis. I don't know if Brianna is my daughter or not, but Alexis told me she was."

Nate had a cold, disturbing look in his eyes. He tried to cover up his whole demeanor by adding a smirk. A shrug followed, then he stroked his chin. "What do you want me to say, Bones? You hurt me, man. I thought you was my boy." He started pounding his fist into his hand. "The one chick who came into my life and rescued me from all of my pain, you had to have her. Not only that, but you also made a baby with her. Then . . . every single day, the two of y'all smile in my face and pretend that everything is all good. You talk all that shit about loyalty and respect, and about how much you got my back. Nigga, please. You ain't got shit. Nothing but a bunch of low-class bitches making a big deal about yo' dick. I lost all respect for Alexis. That's why every time I look at her, I want to beat her muthafucking ass! Every time I see you, all I can think about is plotting yo' demise. I want you to feel my pain, and it will be my pleasure when that day arrives. It looks like we're standing in the moment."

Nate removed a gun from his jacket, then aimed it at me. I didn't know what to do. Felt bad about what I'd done, no doubt. Saying I was sorry seemed inappropriate right now. My eyes shifted to the gun, then over Nate's shoulder where I could see Red standing calmly.

"Stop this, Nate," she said in a calm tone. "This shit ain't worth it. I don't want nobody to get hurt, and I'm sure Bones regrets all that happened in the past. It was a long time ago, and as boys, y'all need to sit down and talk that shit out."

Nate swung around and tilted his head slightly to the side. "Bitch, shut the fuck up. Now all of a sudden, this nigga some kind of saint to you. All it takes is some good ol' dick, before you hoes start singing a new tune. And since you want to open yo' big fucking mouth, let me tell Bones what you've really been up to." Nate pivoted back to me and darted his gun at me as he spoke. "See, you think these bitches be down with you and shit, but all they really want is orgasms and money. Nigga, I paid this ho to fuck you. I paid her to seduce you, and sooner or later—"

"Stop lying!" Red shouted. "That's not how it went down, and you know it! I told you that I didn't want anything to do—"

While still facing me, Nate reversed the gun and put it on his shoulder. He aimed it in Red's direction. "One more word and I swear that I will blow yo' goddamn brains out! Speak again, bitch!"

Red opened her mouth, but no words were spoken. She kept shaking her head no, mouthing to me that he wasn't telling the truth.

Nate turned the gun to me again. The only reason I hadn't made a move yet was because I wanted to hear him out, and I wanted to know where Brianna was. "Anyway," he continued, "she was going to drug you. Drug you, man, and then call me so I could come finish the job. I've been fucking her ass all along, and the only reason you ain't six feet under right now is because she demanded more money from me. Can you believe that shit? This bitch wanted more money! I hope like hell that you didn't fall for the bullshit. If you did, I'm hella sorry that yo' feelings are probably hurt."

"Not hardly," I said. "And if killing me is going to make all of yo' troubles magically disappear, then go ahead and do it. I'm not afraid to die. If anyone should know that, it's you."

Red was still behind Nate, trying to quietly make a move. He chuckled, and without looking in her direction, he lifted the gun over his shoulder again and fired. The bullet shattered glass on her entertainment center, causing Red to duck and stop in her tracks.

"Don't move!" Nate barked.

I wasn't about to try to talk some sense into him. The damage was already done. And even though he was adamant about killing me, he seemed to want to get a lot off his chest.

"Where's Brianna?" I asked calmly.

Nate swallowed hard, then shut his eyes. He pretended to display hurt, but hidden away in the darkness of his eyes was glee. He touched his chest, then squeezed it. Faking as if he was choked up, his voice cracked. "Ya . . . Y'all made me hurt her. I . . . I didn't want to. I swear I didn't, and she just didn't understand how her own daddy could do something like that to her." His face straightened, and a tiny smirk appeared. "Then again, I'm not her real father, am I?"

My blood levels boiled over. I didn't know if he was being truthful or not, but his words were enough for me to put his ass out of his misery. But before I made my move, Nate backed up and pressed the gun against his temple. He tilted his head and left me with a crooked smile. "Now, you must live with yo' betrayal, and suffer the consequences of what it caused. See you in hell, my nigga."

He pulled the trigger and blew his own fucking brains out. I stood for a moment, unable to move. Seeing his brains splatter and his twisted body that dropped back on the couch made me ill. All I could hear was Red crying. She kept yelling for me to call 911, because she didn't know where her phone was. I couldn't do much. Everything was a blur. It wasn't supposed to go down like this. Who in the hell ordered my steps? I was beyond hurt. Destroyed. I staggered over to Nate, barely able to look at him. Red rushed up to me and threw her arms around my neck.

"I'm soooo sorry," she cried out. "Bones, I never meant for any of this to happen. I wanted to tell you about Nate, but I didn't think you would believe me. I know what you did to him was wrong, but you and I aren't responsible for this. Nate was a bully. He was an animal, and you can't deny what kind of person he was!"

Red hadn't said anything that I hadn't already known. Nate was all of that, and then some. But then again, so was I. I pulled away from Red and removed her arms from around my neck. I searched deep into her sad eyes, then softly rubbed my finger against her smooth, chocolate skin. I rubbed her sexy lips, and when my eyes shifted to them, she leaned in for a kiss. This time, I couldn't resist. I sucked her lips with mine and invited her tongue into a sweet dance. She moaned. I moaned. My hands roamed underneath her silk robe, and I massaged every inch of her meaty ass. I swallowed her saliva, and as my dick began to get hard and attempt to escape from my jeans, I halted our intense kiss. She smiled, and as my hands now comforted her face, she slowly shut her eyes.

"I think I'm falling in love with you," she whispered, then opened her eyes to receive my response. I responded with a blank expression. Then, in less than a few seconds,

I snapped her head to the side, breaking her fucking neck. I didn't stay around to see her body drop to the floor, but I damn sure heard a loud thud. While I believed Red had fallen for me, I couldn't ignore her lies.

With a heavy heart, I returned to Nate's house with bad news. Alexis saw the look in my eyes as I casually walked up the driveway.

"Please, God, nooooo," she said, running up to me. "Please don't tell me that nigga hurt my baaaaby! He didn't hurt my baby, did he?"

She pounded my chest, and with no response from me, she dropped to her knees. "Nooooo, Bones, nooooo! Please, nooooo!"

I looked down at Alexis who was rocking back and forth on her knees. Tears streamed down her face. I wanted to console her, but couldn't. I was dealing with too much right now my damn self.

"Sorry I couldn't bring her home," I said in a whisper, and then walked off.

Alexis hollered after me. "Bones! Whyyyy? Where is she? Did you see her? Did he kill her?"

I wasn't sure yet, but the amount of blood that I'd seen in the trunk of Nate's car implied that he had done something bad to Brianna. If so, I needed to find her body. I also had an urge to go see Theo. Maybe Mango would get his wish. Something inside told me that the rest of my day wouldn't get any muthafucking better.

BONES

Sadness was trapped in my eyes. Brianna was in my thoughts. I didn't know where she could possibly be until I parked my car in front of Theo's house. There Brianna was, running around in the yard and playing with two other kids. A sigh of relief came over me. Thank God she wasn't dead. I wanted to call Alexis right away to let her know Brianna was good. Alive. But instead, I had to let her sweat for a little while. She was the one who had put us all in this fucked-up situation, and even though I took part of the blame, still, if it wasn't for her, we wouldn't be here. Nate . . . dead. Red . . . dead. I had to do what I had to do pertaining to her, but I was still in shock about Nate killing himself. Damn. That was fucked up. The thoughts of what went down would stick with me. I was sure that was his purpose.

By now, I figured the police were swarming Red's place. It looked like a murder-suicide, if you asked me. That was how I intended to spin it, and unfortunately, Nate had to go down as a crazy-ass nigga who couldn't control himself. I was almost sure that Alexis would tell the same story, if she was questioned. And as soon as I finished my business with Theo, the plan was to check back in with Alexis to make sure she told the police everything they needed to know.

I flicked a cigarette butt out the window, then opened the car door. The kids Brianna kept playing with were still running around, but she stopped running to look at me. My heart went out to her. She had no idea what had happened to the man she had known as her father, and it was a shame that she was born into this fucked-up situation. While something inside told me she was my daughter, I still wasn't sure. I intended to get a DNA test done pronto.

"Is my daddy with you?" Brianna asked with a bright smile. "He dropped me off earlier and said he would be right back."

I took a hard swallow, then reached for her hand. "Naw, your daddy ain't with me. I'ma take you home in a little bit though. I need to go inside and holla at your uncle Theo for a few minutes. Is he in there?"

Brianna nodded. I gave her a piece of gum that was in my pocket and told her to finish playing with her friends. With Brianna around, I wasn't sure how I was going to handle Theo. But he was the one who had spilled our secret and told Nate me and Alexis had been fucking.

The door was already open. I slowly walked inside, and there was Theo to my left, sitting on a raggedy-ass leather couch. The stench of marijuana was in the air, and for a nigga to consider himself a hustler, his crib looked like crap. His hands were behind his head, and with his shirt off, his skinny chest showed. Without a blink, he stared at me from behind his nerdy glasses.

"I already know why you here, Bones. But before you say one word, you gotta take responsibility for what you did too. Nate deserved to know the truth. I didn't feel right keeping a secret like that on lock."

"If you felt it was gon' be a problem for you to keep our secret, then you should have come to me and said something. Nate had been harboring those ill feelings for a long fucking time. Now it has come to this. I don't know why he brought Brianna over here to you, but I guess he probably told you that he was coming after me."

Theo sat up straight, then clenched his hands together. A slow nod followed. "Yeah, he told me. I wanted to warn you, but I decided to fall back and stay out of it. Y'all need to handle this shit—squash it and let's be done with it. All of this over that bitch Alexis ain't worth it."

Obviously, he didn't know what Nate had done. I had to break the news to him, so I took a few steps forward and eased my hands into my pockets.

"Nate is out. He killed himself a few hours ago in Red's apartment. It's too late for us to squash anything. Had you said something to me sooner, maybe I could've dealt with the shit."

Theo's eyes bugged. His face twisted. He slowly removed his glasses, then placed them on the table. He sucked in a deep breath while shaking his head.

"Nate wouldn't have ever killed himself, so, nigga, quit lying. What did you do to him, fool? Did you kill him so that you and that bitch Alexis could hook up? He said you would do some shit like this. He sholl told me."

I didn't appreciate how Theo was getting at me, so my voice went up a notch. "Fuck Alexis. I don't know why you sitting there making this about her when it ain't. Nate did this to himself. Don't blame me for him not being able to deal with his shit!"

Theo's eye twitched. I could tell he was about to make a move on me. "I swear, if I don't do nothing else, I'ma make sure yo' ass go down for this. You going down, Bones, and I mean that shit."

Theo charged off the couch and tried to rush me. His attempt failed. Within seconds, I had him twisted like a pretzel while yelling for him to calm the fuck down.

"Now, nigga, or else! Chill the fuck out!"

"Or else *what?*" he said, trying to wiggle away from my tight grip. "You gon' kill me too?"

"I damn sure thought about it, all the way here! And if you think I killed Nate, that's too fucking bad. Nigga, *you* killed Nate! The day you told him about me and Alexis, *you* killed him!"

I shoved Theo's punk ass away from me. He stumbled and almost fell on the floor. Catching his balance, though, he hurried to stand up. His narrowed eyes shot daggers at me.

"You ain't shit, Bones. Get the fuck out of my crib before I do something I know I'ma regret."

I stepped forward and stood face-to-face with him. "I don't do well with threats, and if you keep on making them, I'ma have to do something about it."

Theo backed away from my aggressiveness. "And I don't do well with niggas who stab their friends in the back, then pretend as if *they're* the victims. Get out of here with that bullshit. I'ma find out what really happened today at Red's crib. And when she tells me how things went down, yo' ass going straight to a jail cell where you belong. That ain't no threat; it's a promise."

"And I'm about to make you a promise too. You will die before that shit happens. Now, I'ma take Brianna back to Alexis. By then, you'd better have yo' head on straight. You'd better think long and hard about how you getting at me, and about what you're accusing me of. I don't like to be accused of shit that I didn't do, so do your homework well."

"Well, somebody did something, and I know for a fact that Nate ain't foolish enough to kill himself. Yo' shit betta check out 'cause I straight feel a war brewing if it doesn't."

This nigga was tripping. War my ass. He wasn't about shit, especially without Nate or me. But even so, I didn't like how he was getting at me. I also figured that I was wasting my time trying to convince Theo that Nate had inflicted his own wounds. That was time I didn't have. I had to get Brianna back to Alexis and see if the police had come by to question her yet.

Ignoring Theo, I made my way to the door. Brianna was on the porch with her friends, so I reached out for her hand.

"Let's go home. Your mama's been looking for you."

Brianna waved good-bye to her friends. As they left the porch, she and I walked to my car. I tightened the seat belt to strap her in, but as I got in on the driver's side, the direction of my eyes shifted to Theo. He stood in the doorway with a gun in his hand. It was aimed in my direction. He mouthed the word, *"Pow"* while displaying a wicked smile. At first, I thought about squashing our beef. But I was already having a badass day. Maybe it was time for me to put complete closure to the past. Mango had asked me to handle Theo for him before, and I was sure that doing so would be very beneficial to me. Besides, we were no longer boys. Hadn't been in quite some time—I had been in denial. Theo was down with Nate. Period. That meant he would come after me, just because. The one mistake that I didn't want to make was letting my enemies live.

I started the car, then increased the volume on the radio. Brianna looked at me with a smile. I smiled back.

"I'll be right back," I said. "I forgot something, so keep the doors locked until I come back."

She nodded, and as soon as I exited the car, she turned the volume higher. I kept my eyes locked with Theo's as I approached the door. The gun was now by his side. He tapped it against his leg while sucking his teeth.

"I couldn't make out what you were saying," I said, then shifted my eyes toward the gun. "You got a bullet in that muthafucka for me?"

Theo stepped back as I entered his crib again. "After I make a few phone calls, I may have two bullets for you, instead of one. Until then, get the fuck out of my crib, you fake-ass nigga."

Talk was cheap. I didn't bother to respond. I kept my eyes on Theo, plotting to make my next move. He backed up again, then raised his gun a few inches. I reached for his wrist to grab it, but in an instant, he pulled the trigger. A bullet went straight through the hardwood floor, missing my foot by inches. I couldn't believe how much Theo had been trying my patience, but he realized how much trouble he was in when I twisted his arm around his neck and forced him to hold the gun steady on the back of his head.

"This . . . This how you gon' do me?" he shouted with spit flying from his mouth. "Kill Nate, then kill me!"

I bent him over to look at the floor. Didn't want to look into his eyes when I blew his fucking brains out. "I didn't kill Nate, but I *am* going to kill you. Then again, you gon' do it."

I squeezed Theo's finger on the trigger, but it wasn't easy to make him pull it. He used every ounce of strength he had to pull my hand away from his, but eventually, his strength was no match for me. The loud pop instantly dropped him, and the gun with his prints on it skidded across the floor. The hole in the back of his head gushed with blood, and as it began to pour down the side of his face, I felt nothing inside. No pain. No remorse. No nothing. And as far as I was concerned, the past was behind me. Or, at least, that's what I'd thought.

ALEXIS

Everything was a blur. My mind couldn't comprehend what the police officer had told me about Nate. He had killed himself, along with two bitches he'd been fucking with over the years. One of the chicks was Red. The other was a chick named Charlene who lived in the same apartment complex as Red. I'd known about both of the hoes, but it just didn't seem like Nate to kill a bitch, put her in the trunk of his car, and then dump her body in a Dumpster. Then again, there were times when I seriously thought that nigga was crazy. Cuckoo and out of his mind. He'd been taking meds for years, and whenever he failed to take them, shit got out of hand. For me to think this day would never come, I had to be a fool. He'd been off for a long time, and since he didn't want to get help, this was the end result. Hell, there were times when I felt as if I needed help too, especially since I'd let Nate get away with many things. No man should've been allowed to do what he'd done to me, and, sadly to say, a part of me was glad that it was over. But even though I was glad, I was still hurt like hell.

I plopped on the couch with tears streaming down my face. My head ached so badly that I squeezed it and applied pressure with my fingertips. My face was pale, and the black eye Nate had given me a few days ago was still visible.

"I . . . I don't know anything about those women," I lied to the police as they questioned me about Red and

Charlene. "All I want to know is where my daughter is. He left here with her, and I have not seen or heard from her. Would somebody . . . anybody please go find her?"

The nice white officer reached in his pocket and pulled out several tissues. He gave them to me after taking a glance at my sexy thighs that could be seen through the short silk robe I wore. I blew my runny nose, then blinked away my flowing tears.

"Thank you," I said softly.

"You're welcome. We're going to do our best to find your daughter, but do you mind if we look around for a bit? We'd really like to know Nate's state of mind for—"

"I can tell you right now that his state of mind was fucked up. He's been off for quite some time, and all we did was fight each other. I don't mind if you look around, but please, please, help me find my daughter. I pray to God that he didn't hurt her too."

The officers said they would only be there for a few more minutes. I watched as they moved around, looking for clues about why Nate would do something like this. His loss was hard for me to swallow. Yeah, we had our heated arguments and fistfights, but there was a time when I loved the hell out of him. Nobody could tell me anything about him. He was my everything . . . until he started putting his hands on me. I figured that he must've known how I felt about Bones too. After what had happened between us years ago, it was difficult for me to shake my feelings for him. There was something about him that made me weak. Weak enough that whenever Bones was around, Nate could read my thoughts like a book. And every time Bones left, I argued and fought with Nate. He accused me of loving Bones, and even though I denied it, the truth was, I wanted to be with him more than I wanted to be with Nate.

As I listened to the officers talking in the other room, I heard the front door open. When I looked up, I saw Bones walk in. He was carrying Brianna, and in an instant, a huge burden felt as if it had been lifted off my shoulders. Brianna's arms were wrapped tightly around his neck, and she was asleep. I hurried off the couch and ran up to them.

"Thank God," I cried out. I removed Brianna from his arms and hugged her tight. "Wha . . . Where was she? I can't believe you found my baby. Thank you, Bones, thank you so much."

He looked toward the bedroom where the police officers were. "Are the police here?" he asked.

"Yes," I said, still holding on tight to Brianna and rocking her in my arms. "And it's not good. I don't know how to tell you this, but Nate shot himself. He killed two other people too, and the police—"

I choked up, thinking about all that had happened. This felt like a dream—A bad one that I couldn't seem to wake up from. I looked into Bones's eyes, and he appeared out of it. He walked sluggishly over to the couch and took a seat. As he massaged his hands together, he stared straight-ahead.

"What else did the police say?" he asked.

I walked further into the room, but remained standing. As I told Bones the details, I also asked him where he'd found Brianna.

"She was, uh, at Theo's crib. Nate must've dropped her off there. She was outside playing with some kids, and he was inside. I asked if he'd known where Nate had gone, but he said he didn't know. After that, I jetted."

"Well, I'm glad that Nate took her over there. I had no idea—"

I paused when the officers came back into the living room. They looked at Bones who was now sitting with his head lowered, looking at the floor.

"I see that your little girl made it home," one of the officers said. "Did he bring her here?"

Bones lifted his head and spoke up. "Yes. Nate dropped her off with me earlier. He seemed out of it, and now I regret not trying to get to the bottom of what was going on with him. I'm a good friend of his. Bones."

Bones stood, then reached out his hand to both officers.

"Bones?" the officer questioned. "What's your birth name?"

I was definitely waiting to hear his response. I never knew what it was, and from what Nate had said, Bones never told anyone. I asked Nate if he knew. He said he did.

Bones cocked his neck from side to side, then licked his lips. "My birth name is Bones."

The officers glanced at each other, and then the same one questioned Bones again. "What's your last name?"

Bones didn't hesitate to respond. "Bones. First name, last name is the same."

One of the officers wanted to push, but when Bones asked if he was being arrested for something and threatened to call his attorney, they backed off and turned their attention back to me.

"Thanks for allowing us to look around without a warrant. Sorry, again, for your loss, and I hope you and your little girl will be okay. If we have any further questions, we'll be in touch."

I slowly nodded, then followed the officers to the door. I felt that they knew something they weren't saying, and the sneaky looks in their eyes alarmed me. I was eager for them to leave because I had a few questions for Bones.

After I locked the door, I took Brianna to her room to lie down. She was knocked out. I gave her several kisses, thanked God again for her safe return, and then made my way back into the living room with Bones. For someone who had just lost a best friend of many years, he didn't seem as moved as I expected him to be. Bones was good at hiding his emotions, but this was Nate. They were boys, and there was a time when they were inseparable.

I leaned against the doorway with my arms folded, trying to read him. "You haven't said much about Nate, and I don't know what made you just lie to that officer. You told him that Brianna was with you. Why didn't you tell them she was with Theo?"

He rubbed his hands together, massaging them. "Because it ain't none of their damn business, that's why. And don't start asking me any questions. I didn't know Nate was out there like that. I feel bad that he felt like that was his only option. Maybe that incident between us fucked with his head more than I thought it did."

"I'm sure it did, but not many people knew Nate had mental issues. He was taking medication for his illness, but something made him snap. Why did he kill Red and Charlene? It must've been something with them too, but I'm so confused right now that I can't even think straight. I need to go make some phone calls and tell his relatives what happened. I'm sure Theo would want to know too, so if you could tell him what went down I would appreciate it. Also, as far as I know, he didn't have a life insurance policy. See what you and Theo can do to help me pay for his funeral."

"Will do," Bones said, then reached into his pocket to get his cell phone.

I left the room to go make several calls. It was painful talking to some of Nate's aunts and cousins. Many of them were in disbelief. They couldn't believe what Nate had done, especially since many of them spoke about how much he loved me and Brianna. Thing is, they were on the outside looking in. As much as Nate kicked my ass, I knew deep down that there was a side to him that hated me deeply. His aunt knew it too. Nate had confided in her more than I thought he had.

"He does have a life insurance policy, and I'll be sure to take care of everything. I'm his beneficiary, and he told me what to do if anything ever happened to him. I don't know if this policy will hold up, considering the suicide, but I will let you know something soon. Meanwhile, see about Brianna and be sure to let her know how much Nate really loved her."

"I will. And thank you for everything. Nate loved you too, and it doesn't surprise me that he trusted you to take care of everything for him."

"Thing is, he didn't trust you. You already know why, Alexis, but I'm not going there right now. Thanks for calling and I'll be in touch soon."

She hung up, and I swallowed hard, thinking about all of the negative shit Nate must have told her about me. I could've given her an earful about him too, but at this point, it wouldn't have done me any good. After speaking with her, though, I felt sick to my stomach. I was disappointed and didn't know if Nate's family would point the finger at me for what he'd done. I wasn't the perfect girlfriend, but I did my best to hold him down. Nobody knew how difficult that was, especially with his womanizing and abusive ways. I started feeling angry about the whole thing. There was no secret that the next few days would be difficult for me to get through.

I went into the bathroom and shut the door. My hair looked a mess, and my eyes were red and swollen from crying so much. I touched the blue and black bruise underneath my eye, thinking about the argument Nate and I had before he left. He disrespected me so badly. Right in front of Brianna. Maybe it was a good thing that he was dead, but what in the hell made him take the lives of two other women? I probably would never know. And to be truthful, I was ready to get his funeral over with and move the hell on with my life.

I dabbed my face with a cold rag, and then tightened the belt on my silk robe. After I turned off the light, I checked on Brianna who was still asleep, then headed to the living room where Bones was on the couch indulged in a conversation. I figured he was speaking to Theo, until I heard him say Mango's name. I was surprised that Bones was speaking to him, because Mango was bad news.

"I'll shoot that way tomorrow. We'll holla then."

Bones nodded, cracked his knuckles, then ended the call. I sat across from him in a chair with my mind racing. "Did you get a chance to holla at Theo yet?"

Bones looked at his cell phone, then touched a few buttons. "Naw, he didn't answer when I called him. I left him a message for him to hit me back, and I also sent him a text. When I left his place earlier, he said he was going to see Nichelle. He's probably with her."

"I have her number somewhere. I'll look for it and call her later. As for the money, Nate had an insurance policy. His aunt doesn't know if it'll pay out on suicides, but regardless, she said everything would be taken care of."

"Good."

Bones looked at the watch on his wrist, then yawned. I was still a bit shocked by his reaction to all of this. He hadn't said much. I guess I was fooling myself if I thought I would see any tears.

"It's been a long day, and it's getting late," he said, stretching his arms and yawning again. "I'm getting ready to make some moves. Can I get you or Brianna anything before I go?"

Lord knows I didn't want me and Brianna to be here by ourselves tonight. Nate's scent was all over the place. I knew I wouldn't get any sleep. Maybe we could go to a hotel or something. Just for a few days. Then again, maybe Bones would be willing to stay and help me get through this.

"I know this may be asking too much of you, but would you please stay the night with me and Brianna? You don't have to sleep in the same bed as me, if you don't want to. I just need to feel safe. With you here, I know I will."

Bones narrowed his eyes and stared at me from across the room. His eyes were so damn sexy and even with a blank expression on his face, he was fine as fuck. I had some naughty thoughts swarming in my head too, and there wasn't a damn thing that I could do to wash them away.

"I'll stay," he said. "But do me a favor and get me a couple of aspirin. I got a banging-ass headache that won't go away."

"I can definitely take care of that for you. And thanks for staying."

I got up to get Bones some aspirin and wound up taking some for my headache too. I then went to the kitchen to get him a glass of water and when I returned to the living room he was lying back on the couch with his arm resting on his forehead. His eyes were closed, and his shirt was off, displaying his muscle-packed body. I stood next to him admiring the jaw-dropping scenery. Probably sensing that I was standing over him, he slowly opened his eyes, then reached for the glass of water.

"Thanks," he said, taking the aspirin. He put them in his mouth, then tossed back the water. After clearing his throat, he gave the glass back to me. "You need to get some sleep tonight. And after you rest, I need to get at you about several things regarding Brianna."

Every time Bones spoke of her, it made my heart race. "Things like what? Whatever you want to know, just ask."

"Not tonight. Been a long day and I'm sure we both could use some sleep."

He was so right about that. But when I went into the bedroom, Nate's presence was everywhere. From the pictures on our nightstand, to his clothes that filled our closet. Even his fluffy pillow on the bed kept my thoughts locked on him. I tucked it between my legs, then closed my eyes. And after lying there for at least an hour, I still couldn't sleep. I tossed and turned, gazed at the ceiling, thought about when we'd first met, and then about our final days together. A part of me blamed myself for making him crazy like that, but I didn't blame myself for making him a womanizer. As I thought about the numerous times he'd cheated on me, those thoughts made me angry. His whorish ways are what drove me to have sex with Bones that day. I wanted revenge, and the only way I felt as if I could get some kind of satisfaction from how badly Nate had treated me that day was by fucking his best friend. I damn sure didn't expect for the dick to be that good though. And I never thought that I would get pregnant either. But it happened. I kept telling myself that there was a chance that Brianna was Nate's child too. When she was born, however, I knew Nate wasn't the father. It was clear as day. She had Bones written all over her.

I started to kick up a sweat, so I tossed the covers aside and slightly opened my robe. Almost immediately Bones came to mind. I thought about his sexy ass lying on my couch. I wondered if he was asleep. I also wanted to check on Brianna again, so I quietly got out of bed and went to her room. She was still knocked out, so I kissed her forehead and pulled up the covers for her to stay warm. I was so thankful that nothing had happened to her. Several hours ago I was about to lose my mind. Bones was right on time when he came through the door with her in his arms. It was a feeling that I would never, ever forget. I owed him big time.

I peeked into the living room, seeing that Bones was still in the same position as he was before. This time, though, all he had on was a pair of compression shorts that tightened on his muscular thighs and ass. His chocolate skin looked smooth and rich. And there was no way for me to ignore his bulge that was sitting high and pretty. His tight abs moved in and out as he breathed. He appeared to be in a deep sleep. I didn't want to wake him, but I was definitely in the mood to feel his arms wrapped around me. I wanted to feel something else too, but I didn't know if he would be willing to venture there with me tonight. Nonetheless, I took my chances and tiptoed over to him.

My eyes scanned down his entire body. Witnessing it up close made me remove the belt from my robe and slide it off my shoulders. I dropped it to the floor and stood naked beside him. Feeling so unsure about this, I didn't know if I should wake him first or just straddle myself on top of him. The last thing I needed tonight was rejection. There was a huge part of me that knew Bones wasn't about to let this go down. I released a deep sigh, deciding to take my horny ass back into the bedroom to deal with my thoughts. But as I bent over to reach for my robe, Bones shifted on the couch.

"What do you want?" he said in a whisper with his eyes still closed. "And why are you standing over me?"

His eyes slowly opened. I slid my robe back on, but it remained opened in the front with my goodies on display. "I . . . I'm not sure what I wanted, but I couldn't sleep. I thought you may have had some trouble sleeping too."

He shrugged. "Nope, I'm good. Haven't slept like this in a while."

That was odd, but, oh well. I only wished that I could get some sleep too. "Well, I'll let you get back to—"

My words halted when Bones reached out for my hand. "Lie down," he said.

I was so caught off guard by his actions. "Lie down where? In my room?"

"No. On me."

"Seriously?"

He pulled me toward him. I didn't hesitate to straddle the top of him, but I had to admit that I was nervous. Bones had always rejected my advances toward him. I wasn't sure why he seemed ready for me now, but I guess he figured, like I did, that no more harm could be done. As our eyes stayed connected, he removed the robe from my shoulders and let it fall back. I was in total shock when he started to massage my breasts together—his touch had my pussy leaking already. I could feel the growth of his muscle between my legs, and my toes curled from the thoughts of him slipping his big dick inside of me. My nipples were harder than rocks and when a slight arch formed in my back, Bones lifted me slightly to remove his shorts. His dick plopped out and stood taller than the first time I laid my eyes on it. I was eager to feel it grow in my mouth, but my pussy needed him more. No matter what my thoughts were, I let him make the next move. It consisted of him directing his dick at the entrance of my cream-filled slit. He inched his way inside, causing me to gasp and fall forward. I tried to silence my whimpering with a kiss on his lips, but as my mouth touched his, he turned his head.

"Do . . . Do you not want to do this?" I strained to say as he began to stroke me. "You act—"

He reached out and placed two fingers over my lips. "Shhh. If I didn't want to do this, I wouldn't be doing it."

He always spoke the truth. And with confirmation that he was onboard with this, I lowered my left foot to the floor, using it for leverage as I began to ride him. My sticky juices covered his shaft, and the feel of his dick painting my walls had me on cloud nine. I could barely contain myself. His meat filled me to capacity and tickled the shit out of my insides. My breasts were in his mouth, and as he switched his attention from one to the other, his strokes remained at a gentle pace.

"I can't believe we're doing thiiiiiis," I moaned. "Do you know how long I've waited to feel this again?"

Bones circled his curled tongue around my nipples. His hands roamed my curves, and he gripped my ass tightly as I grinded hard on him. My mouth was wide open. Saliva dripped from one corner, so I licked across my lips to catch it. Bones was still working my breasts, and wanting so badly to kiss him, I removed my titty from his mouth and lifted his head. As I leaned in to his lips, he turned his head.

"Why won't you let me kiss you? I want to taste your lips. Please let me taste them."

He cocked his neck from side to side, and I heard it pop. "No," he said, then eased his dripping wet steel out of me. A flood of my creamy juices ran down the crack of my ass, and I thought we were finished until he got up and kneeled behind me. We resumed in a doggy-style position where he was definitely getting the best of me. And after a while, I could barely catch my breath. I wanted to cry from his hard, deep thrusts inside of me. The fast pace he had chosen weakened me. Our bodies dripped with sweat, and with my head lowered, I became dizzy from trying to meet his strokes. Strokes that made my insides even wetter. That made me come all over him. That made me want him even more, and that made me scream out his name and express my satisfaction. There was no doubt that he had me exactly where he wanted me. I was spent. Had melted like butter right before him.

Damn near wanted to tell him that I loved him, but more than anything, I loved what his dick was doing to me. Loved how he made me feel. Appreciated the touch of his warm hands all over my body. Welcomed the attention he continued to give my breasts, but was disappointed that he didn't want to kiss me. That was why this position worked for him. He didn't have to look at me, nor did he have to subject himself to kissing advances. And even though I wanted one, I couldn't complain. He was fucking me so well that a kiss didn't matter right now. It had been a long time since I'd felt satisfied like this, and even though Nate was probably somewhere watching us, I couldn't resist the opportunity of being so up close and personal with Bones's dick again.

Almost ready to throw in the towel, I fell forward with my ass still hiked in the air. Bones had my cheeks spread far apart while he glided in and out of my simmering heated pocket. I closed my eyes and took deep breaths. Could feel another orgasm on the way, and as I felt his balls smack my ass and his fingers manipulate my clit, I let him have it. I locked my pussy on his shaft, then squirted.

"This . . . This shit can't be happening! Plu . . . Please tell me I'm not dreaming. This ain't no dream, is it?" I whined, then dropped my face on a pillow to silence my loud scream. Unfortunately, Bones didn't appreciate my reaction. He grabbed the back of my hair and yanked my head back so tight that I squeezed my watery eyes. I felt his dick deflate and squirm out of me.

"I'm glad you enjoyed yourself, but here's the deal." He spoke in a stern voice. "I want to know if Brianna is really my daughter. I need some legal documents that confirm it either way. You got three weeks to let me know what's up, and if you don't take action, there will be major consequences. Until then, I don't want to hear from you, and

I don't want to see you. If I attend Nate's funeral, don't say shit to me. As a matter of fact, don't even look my way. I'm done with you, and whatever you do, don't you ever offer me this pussy again because I *will* reject it."

He pushed my head forward, then released his tight grip. Yet again, I was shocked. Bones was a trip. One minute he was with it; the next minute he wasn't. I intended to have a paternity test done, but why did he have to be so mean to me? He quickly stood up, and so did I. I blocked his pathway to the bathroom by standing in front of him.

"You don't have to be so cold toward me. I will get you the information you want, and when all is said and done, you'll know for a fact that Brianna is your daughter. Maybe then you can have a little bit more respect for me and you will start to see that us being together ain't as bad as you think. What do you think about that?"

Bones gazed straight into my eyes without a blink. "I think that the only reason you're alive right now is because of Brianna. I wouldn't want to see her in the wrong hands if something ever happened to you, and going forward, she should be your only focus. Just get me what I asked for. After that, we'll go from there."

He walked around me, then went into the bathroom. After closing the door, I heard water running. What he'd said weighed heavily on my mind. Even though I was 110 percent sure about Brianna, 1 percent of me knew that there was a chance of another man being her father. I shook my head, thinking about what I had gotten myself into and the sneaky ways I could get myself out of it. When it involved Bones, I was sure that lying to him wouldn't be easy.

BONES

I sat at the long glass table with Mango sitting next to me. My eyes were locked on a briefcase filled with paper. He displayed a wide smile, showing a grill that cost him a fortune. His pride made me feel kind of good. Kind of like the way a father could make his son feel. This was my promotion. This was for all of the work I had done. Killing Theo proved to Mango that I was capable of doing much more. He was ready to take things to new heights.

He patted my back, then passed me two cigars. "You got big balls, Bones. I like how you move. Love how you keep things to yourself, and I appreciate the fact that you don't let niggas, who are supposed to be close to you, stand in the way. Theo got what he deserved. And the truth is, if you didn't lullaby his ass, somebody else would have. He was a snake. A flunky, and in no way had he been loyal to you. What I'm saying is, I hope you don't have any regrets."

I didn't, but I wasn't about to say it. All I did was listen to Mango. I was more interested in what was next. He kept talking about moving up the ladder, but so far, all he was doing was riding my nuts.

"You are the man. The perfect one to handle some of my business on the outside. I trust only you to do it. You're the one who knows how to get the job done. So, I hope you like to travel. Maybe even travel to places you've never been. My connects come from all over the world, and I'm thrilled to finally have a nigga like you on my team. Other than this money, is there anything else I can get you? Some pussy, more cigars, a car . . . just tell me. I gotta take care of my number one man."

Mango was full of shit, but I liked this nigga. He was real. Didn't hold back and spoke his mind. "The money is good, and whatever you dish out is cool with me," I said. "Just tell me more about this new gig."

Mango cleared his throat, then wiped his hand across his mouth. He stood and walked over to the bar in the far corner of the room, filled a crystal glass with Cognac, then washed it down his throat.

"Ahhhh," he said. "That's some good shit. But in reference to the new gig, I want to utilize yo' skills in a more productive way. I thank you for shaking niggas up and forcing them to do right by me, but there are plenty more muthafuckas out there who are prohibiting me from being all that I can be. Those people need to be dealt with from time to time. With you and Pebbles out there handling things for me, people will begin to respect me and my organization more. They will think twice before fucking me over, and a lot more money can swing my way. More opportunities will arise, and we all could be sitting extra pretty."

"I get a feeling that more murders will be involved. And who is Pebbles?"

"Murder is a nasty word. You won't be murdering anybody, unless you feel a need to. I'd like to think of it as you *handling* things for me. Pebbles is a bitch without a conscience. She has worked for me for the past five years, but I need someone like you to go along with her and make her a little softer. Some of my connects are turned off by her. They would love to see someone like you in the field with a calmer head. Some of them niggas love her to death too. That's why I don't want to let her go."

I glanced at the money slipping through the cracks of the suitcase, then sat up straight. "When I work, I work alone. The last thing I need is a cocky bitch standing in the way of me getting things done."

"She won't get in the way. I already told her about you, and she's willing to work with you. Keep in mind that behind every productive and successful man is a woman. We need to roll like this, and if you ain't feeling it after a month or two, then I'll change plans."

I honestly didn't like where Mango was going with this. He went on and on about how much the police had his back, and with many officers on his payroll, he claimed we were good. Seemed like with the snap of his finger, he made issues like the one with Skittles go away. According to him, there would be no follow-ups about Nate, Theo, or even Red's death because Mango knew how to silence the police. Yet again, he claimed to have my back, and he invited Pebbles to come over so we could meet.

"I'm pulling up right now," she said through the intercom. "I hope you got that for me too."

"Always. You know daddy gon' take care of you. No worries."

Mango walked off, then came back with a Michael Kors purse in his hand. He put it on the table, then told me to tuck away the suitcase.

"I don't want her to see how much I've been giving you. Bitches always complaining about equal rights and equal pay, but we both know that men and women are on different levels. Keep that between us, 'cause the last thing I need is her to get sensitive over that shit."

I stood, tucked the money away in the suitcase, then locked it. Since I had to take a leak, I excused myself from Mango and told him I'd be right back. I took a quick leak, then washed my hands. While looking in the mirror, I cocked my cap sideways, straightened my goatee with the tips of my fingers, then zipped the jacket to my white-and-black sweat suit. I wiped my hands on a towel, then exited the bathroom. Before I made it back into the other room, I could hear a female's sassy voice. She overtalked Mango who was asking her to chill out and calm down.

"At the end of the day," he yelled, "I told you not to shoot him. Yo' ass been trigger-happy lately, and I keep telling you that you need some dick in yo' life to help calm you down."

"Fuck dick. That nigga didn't pay up, so he got what he deserved. You know I don't play that shit, so I don't know why you're so upset with me for following your orders."

"I didn't order you to shoot him. I told you to let Jake handle him. But it's too late now. What's done is done."

From a short distance, I saw Pebbles. She was skinny like Rihanna, but model-like tall. Her body seemed fit for the runway, and the unique leather dress she wore hugged her small curves like a tight glove. Her breasts were tiny, but the size of her ass was round and perfect. I could tell she worked out, and even though she was toned, I definitely appreciated chicks with a little more meat on their bones. Her short, layered haircut was neatly lined, and without a drop of makeup on, her cocoa-brown skin glistened. Her doe-shaped, light brown eyes were luring, and the high arch in her brows classified her as one in a million. I wasn't sure how I felt about working side by side with her, but my dick thumped a little to let me know *it* was feeling her, even if I wasn't. Mango looked past her to speak to me.

"I know you have to get going, but I wanted the two of you to finally meet. Bones, this is Pebbles. I'll hit you up in about an hour or so to let you know our next move. Gotta make a few calls first."

Pebbles swung around to look at me. Her smile vanished. With a blank expression covering her face, she searched me from head to toe, then turned back around. "50 Cent looks better, but that's just my opinion. Anyway, Mango, we need to take care of some things. Let me know when you're done with Mr. Bones."

"We're done," I said, walking up to the table and removing the suitcase. "Go ahead and handle y'all's business." I held out my hand to Mango, and he grabbed it. "Thanks, man. I really do appreciate this. But for the record, my grandmother in a cat suit looks better. That's just my opinion, and I now understand why you're having issues with getting the job done."

Mango snickered as I walked away. Pebbles yelled after me. "Nigga, yo' grandmother wish she could look this good! Get the fuck out of here with that mess and please don't get me started."

I didn't bother to respond. It was already evident that this bitch and I wouldn't get along. I intended to keep my distance, and she would only be useful to me if I started to see some potential.

About an hour later, I sat at my grandmother's house eating dinner. Church music echoed in the background, and the smell of soul food was in the air. She was at the table too, and as she cut into a sweet potato pie and put a slice on my plate, she tried to convince me to move out.

"I know we've had this talk before, Bones, but it's time. You stay here because you worry about me, but I'll be okay. You have your whole life ahead of you, and I don't want you always cooped up in here with me. Besides that, I want to invite my boyfriends over here. You always in the way of me doing things that I want to do."

I smiled, knowing that my grandmother was only teasing me. The last man she invited over here was about ten years ago. I scared him away and almost beat his ass because he was being disrespectful to her.

"You don't have any boyfriends, so stop talking that mess. And I do worry about you. I stay because I want to. I'm comfortable here, and this is home for me. It always will be."

"It will continue to be home, even after you move out. It ain't an option no more. Time for you to leave the nest. I won't start preaching about how uncomfortable I am with all of this sudden money you've been branging in here, and I know you don't want to hear it. By having yo' own place, you can do whatever you wish. I just don't want you to do it while you here."

I wiped my mouth with a napkin, then guzzled down my water. "Are you kicking me out? Is that what you're doing?"

My grandmother winked at me. "Something like that, but in a good way, of course. You can visit as much as you'd like, and I won't even ask you to return my key."

I chuckled and shook my head. I knew this day would come, but I had to find a place that was suitable and close by. I told my grandmother that I would check out of her place, and less than a week later, I had. I found a simple loft with two bedrooms and two bathrooms. It set me back several grand, but with the money Mango had already dished out, I had plenty to spare. As I was carrying a bag of clothes up the spiral stairs that led to my bedroom, my cell phone rang. It was Alexis. I didn't answer, but she sent me a text message saying that we needed to talk soon. Minutes later, Mango called. This time, I answered.

"I want you to meet with Pebbles tonight. She'll give you details about what to do, and it would please my heart if y'all can jet to Atlanta and take care of things for me on Friday."

"I don't know the details, but I have no plans this Friday. Where am I supposed to meet Pebbles?"

"Call her. I'ma give you her number. She'll tell you where she wants to meet."

"That's cool, but to be honest, I can tell that I'ma have some problems with this chick. We won't click. She trying to be boss, and I don't like that shit."

"I feel you on everything you just said, but once you get to know her, you'll see that she's good people. Real sweet. She comes off as being hard and shit, but she soft as a kitten. Just give it some time, and focus on what's important. Business."

Mango gave me her number. I jotted it down, then continued to take my clothes to the walk-in closet. While the loft was simple and empty, it was definitely a step up from my grandmother's crib. The stainless steel appliances, granite-topped island, and tinted windows that viewed the city of Chicago, truly made a nigga feel like he had arrived. I intended to furnish the place, but with as little furniture as possible. More than anything, I needed a bedroom set. The one at my grandmother's house wouldn't do.

While checking out the view, I leaned against the picture windows to return Alexis's call. She answered right away.

"Whenever you get time, I need you to go to this address so they can get a sample of your DNA. Do you have a piece of paper and pencil handy?"

"Text me the info. I'll go tomorrow. And just so you know, I'll be having my own test done too."

"Are you saying that you don't trust me?"

"That's exactly what I'm saying."

"Good. I don't trust you either. Especially since you didn't show up at Nate's funeral. And I know you heard about what happened to Theo too. Why haven't you returned any of my phone calls? Something is up, and I think you know more than what you're saying. I would really like to know what actually happened between you, Nate, and Theo."

"I can't tell you what I don't know, but I didn't show up because I figured Nate wouldn't have wanted me there. As for Theo, I'm disappointed. Didn't know that he didn't value his life either. What a shame."

"Bones, that's bullshit, and you know it. You know this mess don't add up, and why would Theo kill himself too? Nichelle has been asking me all kinds of questions about that day. She wants to talk to you as well."

"Fuck Nichelle or anybody else who thinks I'm involved. You lucky that I'm still talking to you, but I have a feeling that our conversations will soon cease. I'm going to Atlanta this weekend. When I come back, I expect some results. No more games, Alexis, just results."

I ended the call with Alexis, then dialed out to call Pebbles. She answered right away too.

"Where do you want to meet?" I asked.

"Who is this?" she snapped.

"Bones."

"Bones who?"

"Bones who ain't got nothing on 50."

"Oh, *that* one. Well, since I don't invite people I don't like to my crib, how about I meet you at a restaurant?"

"Sounds good to me, especially since you can stand to eat a little something. Choose a place with greasy, fatty foods. Somewhere you can get some desserts to help enhance a few things. Then again, where we eat is your choice, not mine."

"Fuck you, Bones, all right? Meet me at Geno's Bar & Grill around six. It's a little hole-in-the-wall, but I'm sure you're used to being in those kinds of places."

She hung up. I wasn't looking forward to meeting with her, but I had to keep in mind what Mango had said. This was all about business. About us making more money.

Money that could set me up pretty and put me on a path I was destined to be on. Only because of that, I went with the flow.

Later that day, I changed into a pair of True Religion jeans and a black hoodie. My hair was trimmed and goatee was shaved perfectly to suit my chin. I snatched my keys from the island, and then left to go meet up with Pebbles. The parking lot was jammed-packed, and the inside was thick with people gossiping, eating, dancing, and drinking. It was stuffy as hell, and the dance floor was no bigger than a ten-by-ten square. All heads turned each time the door opened, and many of the women, both young and old, had their eyes on me. I tossed my head back and kept it moving to an empty booth I spotted near the restroom. It was only big enough for two people, but it was the only place I could find to sit. I hadn't spotted Pebbles yet, but I kept looking at my watch because she was late. It was already ten minutes after six. If she wasn't here by six thirty, I was leaving.

As a thick cloud from people smoking filled the air, I waved my hand in front of my face to clear it. I had no problem with the weed smell, but it was very overpowering. A waitress approached the table with pen and paper in her hand.

"What can I get you?" she asked.

"I'm waiting on someone, but a shot of Henny would be good."

"Would you like any appetizers while you wait? We have wings, pulled pork sandwiches, onion rings, and much more. Look over the menu and I'll be back with your drink."

I picked up the menu from the table, and the waitress walked away. As I looked toward the door, two ladies at the bar were trying to get my attention. They waved. I winked, then opened the menu to look at it. Right then, my phone rang. It was Pebbles, but I didn't answer because she was supposed to be here. She sent me a text message saying she was outside searching for a parking spot. Hopefully, she'd find one soon.

Minutes later, I looked at the door and saw her strut in. This time, she rocked a pair of tight leather leggings that looked melted on her skin. The shirt that she wore showed part of her midriff, and her high heels made her even taller. She looked real classy, and there was something about her big doe eyes that made up for how skinny she was. I saw her squinting and searching around for me. When her eyes moved in my direction, I tossed my head back. She proceeded my way displaying nothing but confidence. Other women checked her out. Jealousy was in their eyes. They whispered and frowned, but she ignored them. Many of the men wanted her, but she had a look about her that said no. No man was good enough. Not even me. She kept it moving my way, sticking out like a sore thumb.

As she neared the table, I could smell her sweet perfume. I saw the tiny gap between her legs and wondered when the last time was that she'd been fucked. Well . . . It probably had been awhile, especially since so much seriousness was washed across her face. She had issues, no doubt, and I suspected that like many women who wore their attitudes on their shoulders, she had nigga problems. One fool reached for her waist, and he caught hell. I couldn't make out what she'd said to him, but her facial expression said it all. *Back the fuck up and if you touch me again you will pay with your life.* I couldn't get past the feistiness, but the direction of my eyes traveled to her curvy ass that suited her small frame. As she approached the table, I shifted my eyes in another direction, as if I hadn't been paying attention.

"I didn't expect for it to be this crowded," she said, sliding into the booth. She placed her designer purse on the table, then opened it to pull out a cigarette. "Were you waiting long?"

I cracked my knuckles, then picked up the small glass with a shot of Henny in it. "Been waiting long enough. Now what's the plan? Mango said you were going to provide me with some specific details about our next move."

"Hold up. Can a sista take a few minutes to get comfortable? I mean, I just walked through the door and sat down. Haven't even ordered a drink yet."

"If you had been on time, you would've had time to order a drink." I looked at my watch again, seeing that it was almost six thirty. "But since you late, I need specifics so I can hurry up and get out of here."

"If you had somewhere else to be, you should have said so. We can always reschedule."

I washed down the Henny, then put the empty glass on the table. After that, I reached into my pocket and pulled out a ten-dollar bill.

"I'm out," I said. "Call me with the details about Atlanta and let me know where I need to be when it's time to roll. Have a drink and enjoy your evening."

Pebbles sat with her mouth wide open. "Are you serious?" I heard her say as I walked away. Her voice was drowned out by the loud music. But when I got outside, she was a few steps behind me.

"You know you got a real bad, ugly-ass attitude," she said. "I don't know what your problem is, and I apologize if I hurt your feelings by saying that 50 Cent looks better than you. I had no idea that my opinion would sting that much."

I didn't respond. Kept it moving to my car, then opened the door to get inside. Pebbles stood outside the door with her hand on her hip. "Text me your address and

I'll pick you up around noon on Friday. You'll hear the details then, and I hope you'll be in a better mood."

"I don't invite people that I don't like to my crib, so no need for me to send a text message. Meet me at Mango's place at noon. If you're late, I'm going alone."

I raised the window, then started the car. Pebbles rolled her eyes at me and had nothing else to say as I drove off. She did, however, send me a text message that invited me to kiss her ass. A picture of it followed thereafter, and then a text that said:

I was mistaken. You do look better than 50, but you will never, ever have his money if you don't change your attitude. Glad we're off to a good start.

I was sure she wanted a reply, but I didn't offer one. But as I drove back home, I couldn't stop thinking about her. Thought about how we were going to make this partners-in-crime thing work and about fucking her. I wanted to throw her legs over my shoulders and show her who the real boss was. She had those eyes a nigga could gaze into and get lost. There was something about her that turned me on, but it had been a long time since both of my heads connected. Then, maybe I was just horny. I'd been depriving myself too much, and I had to come clean about how relieved I felt when I busted a nut with Alexis. I could always get my shit off with her, so instead of going home, I drove to her crib. Almost immediately, I noticed several trash cans outside with Nate's things inside of them. I guessed Alexis was cleaning her house out and ridding herself of their fucked-up relationship.

It was a little past seven when I knocked on the door. The porch light came on, and shortly thereafter, Alexis opened the door. She looked surprised to see me. Her hair was pulled into a sleek ponytail, and the jeans she wore were unbuttoned. A tank shirt covered her meaty breasts, and a small container of ice cream was in her hand.

"What's up?" she said, seeming slightly annoyed by my presence.

"Is Brianna here?"

"No. She's with her cousins. Why?"

I opened the screen door, then made my way inside. Alexis continued to watch me with a puzzled look on her face. "Why are you here, Bones?"

"Do you have company?"

"No, I don't. I was watching TV and eating this ice cream."

"Good. 'Cause I came here to eat something too and take care of your pussy since I failed to do so the last time I was here. Take off your clothes."

Alexis's eyes grew wide and looked as if they were about to break out of their sockets. "Huh? Stop playing, Bones. What is this about?"

I pulled the hoodie over my head, then tossed it on the floor. As I reached for the button on my jeans, Alexis kept her eyes locked on me.

"Are you gon' make me ask again? I said, take off yo' clothes."

She dropped the container of ice cream, and within one minute, our clothes were history. Alexis was on the dining room table with her legs spread wide open. Her long nails scratched my back as I forced my tongue inside of her and lightly licked against her walls. The sweet taste of her pussy made me think of Pebbles, and as I fucked the shit out of Alexis, sweating hard and trying to relieve all that was inside of me, I couldn't help it that she wasn't the one trapped in my thoughts.

PEBBLES

Bones and I were finally in Atlanta. We argued most of the way here, or should I say . . . We couldn't agree on much. If I said stop, he said go. If I said, yes, he said, no. If I said this way, he'd say that way. He was a serious pain in my ass, but from the first time I saw him, I liked what I saw. I loved his no-nonsense attitude. Loved how he carried himself, and I loved how I couldn't read him. The mystery made him so attractive to me, and I needed a man like him in my corner. I wasn't sure about anything evolving between us, because he had already made it clear that I wasn't his type. And every time the opportunity presented itself, he let snide remarks slip about my weight. To me, I wasn't too thick or thin. I was perfect, and nothing but healthy foods went into this body. My feelings were slightly bruised from his remarks, but to hell with a nigga who didn't appreciate a woman in good shape. Obviously, he didn't, so that only meant he would be good for having my back.

Pertaining to business, I'd been handling some of Mango's dirty work for years. He had several connects in almost every major city, and whenever business deals needed closure, negotiations had to be made, or some-body had to be killed, Mango turned to me. Whatever he ordered me to do, I did it. His instructions were always precise, but he was a little upset with me for doing shit my own way and not following orders. It had been that way lately because some of the men I stepped to had

gotten cocky and gotten out of line. Just because I was
a woman, it didn't mean I had to put up with anybody's
shit. I didn't, so Mango felt as if adding Bones to the
mix would be best. That was his choice, and thus far, I
wasn't sure if it was a good thing or not. Why? Because
Bones's attitude was just as bad as mine. He had the
capabilities to rub muthafuckas the wrong way too. It
wasn't as if they would appreciate his presence more than
mine, but maybe I was wrong. After all, Carmen seemed
to appreciate Bones. And as we sat on a soft white leather
sectional in her exquisite living room, she was all smiles.
Her dimples were on display as she sat close to Bones,
damn near on his lap. She was a wealthy, beautiful
Puerto Rican woman with megapower. She and I didn't
click, and quite frankly, neither did she and Mango. But
there was no time for petty shit when business was the
priority.

"Remind me to call Mango and thank him for sending
you," she said to Bones with her tanned legs crossed over
his lap. "I think these new negotiations will work out just
fine. The two of you can pick up the package tomorrow
around noon. And if you have time, Mr. Bones, I'd like to
show you around. And just so you know, I won't take no
for an answer."

Bones displayed a fake smile. I could tell he wasn't
with it. He stood, then planted a soft kiss on her cheek.
"I do have some other things planned for tomorrow, but
maybe I can find an hour or two to take a tour. If not
tomorrow, certainly some other time."

Carmen was persistent. People with money and power
always were. "Tomorrow it is. Hopefully, whatever else
you have planned can wait."

Bones knew when to keep quiet. All he did was nod.
We made our way to the double door, and after sealing
one of the deals we drove to Atlanta to close, we got in the

car. It was a rented Mercedes-Benz. Bones drove off, and as we waited for the gates to open, he looked at me.

"Is she always like that," he said.

"Yes. And you'd better stop to pick up plenty of condoms for tomorrow. Her intentions are to fuck your brains out. If she could have done it today, I'm sure she would have."

"All I'm doing tomorrow is picking up the package. That sex bullshit can wait for another day. Besides that, she didn't move me. Sexy as fuck, but too in control and demanding."

I pursed my lips and quickly shot down his comment. "What's wrong with a woman being in control and demanding what she wants?"

"Nothing. But it's all about how you do things. I wasn't feeling her."

That didn't surprise me. Bones wasn't feeling anybody. I could already tell that he was on this mission for money, control, and power. Nothing or no one else mattered. He stayed focused and when we reached our second destination, I let him handle a situation that had gotten out of control. Mango was called last week to send somebody to handle it. In return, he sent the best of the best.

We followed behind Keith who was Big L's right-hand man. Like always, they never wanted blood on their hands, and the dirty work was left for someone like me to do. According to Big L, no one would ever suspect me. I resided in a different state, and Big L didn't have the police on lock in Atlanta like Mango did in Chicago. Here, it was harder to hide crimes, and investigations would definitely take place. People would get questioned, but leads would lead to nothing. Crimes would go unsolved, maybe even for the two pretty white chicks who had snitched. Bones and me were sent there to get names. They weren't talking, and Big L didn't want them to see any familiar faces.

Keith led us to a damp basement that had drips of water coming from the cracked concrete. Behind a wooden door with several locks on it were two white chicks tied to chairs with rope. Their eyes were covered with black blindfolds, and the smell of shit infused the air. A puddle of piss sat beneath their feet, and bruises covered their faces. Dirty socks were stuffed in their mouths and their clothes were shredded. I honestly couldn't tell if they had been raped or not, so I quickly turned to Keith's big and black, yellow-toothed ass.

"Mango sent us here to take care of this for Big L. Why are they down here looking like this?"

"Because the bitches kept on yakking, ignoring me, and talking shit."

"So you had to rip off their clothes and fuck them? Really?"

Keith frowned, then laughed at how upset I was. He was another nigga that I didn't get along with. "Bitch, you were sent here to question *them*, not *me*. Do yo' damn job or take yo' dumb ass back home."

I stepped forward, but Bones grabbed my waist and pulled me back. "Trust me," I said. "I got yo' bitch. And one of these days, she gon' show up and make yo' black fat ass eat your words."

"I'll be waiting on her arrival."

Bones backed me into a corner and stood in front of me. "Chill," he said. "Your temper is too up there. Let no one see you sweat, and you gotta learn to ignore people who don't deserve your attention. Words only hurt if you let them. Now, shake that shit off, and let's get this done."

I rolled my eyes, then turned my head to the side to look at Keith. He irked the fuck out of me, but Bones was right. I don't know what had gotten into me lately. Every little thing set me off, but I needed to chill.

Bones told me to remove the blindfolds from one of the chick's eyes while he removed the blindfold from the other. Both of their faces were almost beet red, and their hair was stringy and matted. It looked as if they'd been in the basement for years, instead of days. I didn't want to get too close because the stench coming from both of them was nothing pretty. After we removed the socks from their mouths, one of them cried out.

"Help us. Can we pleeease go home? This is all a mistake. We never meant to cause anyone any harm."

Keith stood in the far corner with his arms crossed against his chest. I leaned against the wall, watching Bones do his thing. He stood right in front of the women with his bowlegs straddled. That sexy mutha had it going on, but I was sure that those bitches didn't give a damn about a fine muthafucka standing before them. They wanted out of here. Fast.

"Calm down," Bones said. "I've been sent here to get to the bottom of what happened, and if y'all can tell me exactly what went down and who is responsible for Kebow and Treasure being arrested, then I will have no problem opening those doors and letting y'all get out of here. All I ask for is the truth. I also want the names of anybody who coaxed you ladies into doing this."

We all listened in as Bones spoke calmly to the two women and got them to reveal how much they were paid to snitch on Kebow and Treasure. Basically, the bitches were used as pawns to bring them down. The chief of police was the main one involved, and these bitches were offered half a million dollars to help bring down Big L's organization. It was an organization that affected Mango too, so none of us wanted that to happen.

"That's all we know," one of the women said with tears flowing down her face. "We didn't want to do it, and when we tried to renege, Chief Blair said he would have us arrested too. So we had to follow through with the plan. I don't know what else we could have done."

Bones nodded and appeared to sympathize with the women. I sure as hell didn't. My thing was, why get involved from the beginning? And if it were me handling this situation, both of these bitches would be already dead. But Mango ordered me to sit still on this one and take notes. That's what I did.

"I'm not sure what else y'all could have done, but the problem is the evidence," Bones said. "Too much evidence out there, and how do I know that if I decide to let y'all go, y'all won't snitch again?"

"We won't. I promise you that we won't. We'll leave this country, for God's sake, and no one will ever hear from us again."

The other woman pleaded too. "No one," she said. "This has been a horrible experience. We had no idea that it would lead to this. If we don't testify, then there is a chance that Kebow and Treasure will go free. You have our word that we will never ever testify."

Bones released a deep sigh, then eased his hands in his pockets. "Yeah, but a black man on trial is never a good thing. We'll deal with Chief Blair, but what if y'all ain't telling me everything y'all know? I get a feeling that y'all holding back on me. Y'all wouldn't do that, would you?"

The two women looked at each other. One took a hard swallow; then she added another name to the mix. "The mayor," she said. "Mayor Damsey is my uncle. He has had several confrontations with Big L, and he wants his organization brought down before he runs for office again. I didn't want to say anything about him because he's family. But he should have never involved us. I hate like hell that he involved us."

The women started to break down even more. Bones looked at me and asked if I had any tissue.

"Hell no," I bluntly said. "And if I did, they sure as fuck wouldn't get it."

One of the bitch's eyes cut me like a knife when she rolled them. I started to intervene, but decided against it. Bones was taking too long with this shit for real. I was getting real impatient, and Keith's presence wasn't helping me either.

"Anything else I should know?" Bones said. "Tell me the best way to reach the mayor and Chief Blair."

They told Bones that on Friday nights, the mayor and chief could normally be found at a strip joint where private parties were held. They gave Bones the address, along with directions.

"That's good. Thanks for the info."

He started to untie the women, and within a few minutes they were freed, as well as shocked. "Are you really going to let us go? Can we leave?"

Bones shrugged. "Why not? Y'all done told me every-thing I need to know, and I assume that by tomorrow, y'all will be tossing back tequilas somewhere in . . . maybe Mexico, right?"

They both looked at each other and nodded. These fake-ass, snitching bitches needed to quit. I could see straight through their lies. Mexico, my ass.

"Yes. Mexico or wherever. Like I said, you'll never see or hear from us again."

Bones looked at Keith. "Unlock the door," he said. "Let them go and make sure they are nowhere to be found tomorrow."

The women rushed behind Keith and made their way toward the door. They only had a few more steps to take before Bones removed the Glock tucked in his jeans and fired off two bullets. One bullet went into the back of one woman's head, and the other bullet went into the other one's neck. Their bodies dropped simultaneously.

Bones looked at me with no remorse whatsoever on his face. "Can you believe that shit? Those bitches didn't even thank me. How in the fuck was I supposed to trust them?"

I let out a soft snicker thinking the same damn thing. We both moved toward the door, and as one of the women squirmed around on the ground, Bones stood over her. She was trying to say something with blood clogged in her throat.

"What's that?" Bones said, then kneeled down beside her. He placed the gun against her temple. "I know. You're in pain, right? Here, let me help you."

He pulled the trigger, causing her brains to splatter. With some of the blood splattered on my high heeled shoes, I stepped over the women and tiptoed my way back up the stairs behind Keith. I asked where the bathroom was, and he pointed to a nearby room that was down the hall. I quickly cleaned myself up, then saw Bones waiting for me by the door. I now had a clear picture of what kind of man I was dealing with. He was smooth. Ruthless. Coldhearted—and knew how to get shit done. He didn't waste too much time, unless it was necessary. I admired him already, and keeping it real, he was my kind of nigga.

Bones and I left and were on our way to take care of things with the mayor and chief. On our way to the strip club, Mango called and congratulated us on doing a good deed. He also asked me to meet with one of his connects who only spoke French. I would do so tomorrow while Bones was with Carmen. I figured that Mango needed me for the job because Bones couldn't speak French or Spanish. I had learned both languages years ago, knowing that it would one day benefit me.

The strip club we went to was indeed private. But Big L made preparations for us to go inside and have access to some of the back rooms where the so-called magic happened. Chief Blair was in the house tonight, but unfortunately for us, the mayor was nowhere to be found. Bones and I would have to come back another time to deal with him. We had strict orders from Mango to be back in Chicago tomorrow. After those two women's bodies washed up in the river, he didn't want us to be nowhere in the vicinity. So after my meeting tomorrow, we had to jet. Carmen wouldn't have time to get a taste of Bones, and I was glad about that.

Bones and I were waiting in a private room where the chief was expected to come in. Presenting myself as one of the strippers, I started to remove my clothes. Bones sat behind one of the curtains that was there for viewing only. We weren't supposed to be able to see him, but he could definitely see us. He could hear us too, and when I waved at him, he told me to quit playing. I laughed, then eased my tight pants down to the floor. Pulled my top over my head, then raked my short hair back with my fingers. As I stood in lace panties and a bra, I wondered what Bones was thinking, if anything. I kept on my high heels, then quickly sprayed my tight abs with a dash of sweet perfume.

"Can you smell me?" I said jokingly to Bones. Like always, he didn't respond.

I was getting ready to say something else, but then the door opened. In walked the red-faced chief who was sloppy drunk. He stumbled my way with a drink in his hand. His eyes were wide like saucers, and he appeared quite pleased to see me standing there with a little of nothing on, waiting for him.

He looked up, then lifted his glass to the sky. "Thank you, God. I knew this was going to be a good night."

He tossed back the drink, then laid the glass on a table that was in front of a chair I invited him to sit in. I straddled his lap, and with a bright smile on my face I began to tease him.

"You're so handsome. I guess I should be thanking God too, and I promise you that this will be a night that you'll *never* forget."

He was giddy as ever. Couldn't wait for me to work him over, and neither could I. Normally, I would be in and out. I didn't waste time with shit like this, but since I knew Bones was behind the curtain watching and waiting for me to do away with this muthafucka, I decided to put on a little show. I eased the tie away from the chief's neck and began to unbutton his shirt. His potbelly was in my way, but I knew how to work around it. As one of my bra straps fell from my shoulder, the chief reached behind me to unsnap my bra. I hated that his filthy hands touched me, but when he pulled the bra away from my breasts, I didn't say a word.

"You're so freaking sexy," he moaned while massaging my breasts. "I've never been inside of a black woman as beautiful as you are. My dick is already busting through my pants. Can you feel it?"

"Of course," I said with a fake smile. "And thanks for the compliments. They motivate me, and I promise to satisfy your needs to the best of my ability."

He dropped his head back and continued to massage my tiny breasts. I moaned while gazing straight-ahead at the curtain, then closed my eyes as if the chief's touch was doing something to me. He lowered his hands to my ass, and as soon as he reached inside of my panties, I stopped him.

"I want to taste you first. Can I taste you, please?"

He slowly nodded and watched without a blink as I stood to remove my panties. I tossed them to him and invited him to take a sniff.

"I'm in love," he said, sniffing my panties, then gazing at my hairless slit. "Your body, daaaamn it, you sexy bitch. I'm gonna put that pussy to work tonight."

"Please do, and keep those compliments coming. I love it."

We both laughed as he put my panties on his head, promising to keep them. I slithered down to the floor and got on my knees. As I removed his leather belt and unzipped his pants, he dropped his head back again. I removed his tiny dick from his boxers, and as I started to stroke it, I saw the curtain move. I shook my head, alerting Bones not to make a move. The chief lifted his head, then opened his eyes. He gently touched the side of my face while gazing into my eyes.

"Your eyes speak volumes," he said. I shifted my eyes to look behind him. But before he had a chance to turn his head, Bones pulled the trigger on the silencer and blew the chief's fucking brains out. He fell out of the chair and crashed to the floor. His blood splattered all over my nakedness. I was highly upset that Bones didn't let me handle this how I wanted to. From the look on my face, he could tell how upset I was.

I lifted my finger and darted it at him. "Mango told *me* to handle him, not you."

"You took too long. Put your clothes on and let's go."

"I don't take orders from you. Who in the fuck do you think you are?"

He cut his eyes at me, then walked off to exit. I used my clothes to wipe some of the blood off of me, and when I looked down at the chief's dead body, all I could do was spit on him. The sight of the nasty fat bastard made me ill.

Hoping that no one saw me, I quietly closed the door, then left from the back exit where Bones was inside of the car waiting for me. I slammed the door, turned to him, and let him have it.

"You can walk off all you want to and not deal with me, but we need to get one damn thing straight. When

Mango sends *me* on a mission to do something, you need to let *me* handle it. I didn't interfere when you took your measly time dealing with those two other bitches, so please respect how I choose to do things. As long as you do that, we won't have any problems."

Bones cocked his neck from side to side and didn't say shit. We rode in silence back to the hotel, and as soon as we got there, he went his way, and I went mine. Earlier while in the car, we agreed to get up around nine to have breakfast. Afterward, I would go on to have my meeting with the Frenchman, Arnaudo. Bones insisted that he wanted to stay with me, and then we would stop at Carmen's place to pick up the package. I wasn't sure if that was still the plan or not, but when morning came, he was at the breakfast table dressed and ready to go. I hadn't gotten much sleep, but for some reason, he looked well rested.

"Have our plans changed for the day?" I asked before taking a seat at the table.

He chewed his eggs and shrugged his shoulders. "Why would they change? We should be on schedule to get out of here at nine thirty and be on our way to your meeting. We'll meet with Carmen at noon. Hopefully, we'll be on the road by one."

I got up to get a bowl of fruit, and then returned to the table. Dark shades shielded my tired eyes, but I could see Bones looking at me.

"What?" I said. "What are you looking at?"

"Your lack of energy. I take it that you didn't sleep well last night. Feeling bad about what you did to the chief, or should I say, what you made me do to him?"

"Don't even go there. And yes, I am tired. Can't wait to get back home, in my bed, and get some rest."

"Then let's go. Besides, what happened to the chief is all over the news. Too many cops hanging around, and I expect for things to get worse around here."

I agreed. And after I downed some orange juice and ate several more pieces of fruit, we left. I gave Bones directions to Arnaudo's place, and yet again, Bones seemed in awe by the immaculate house that looked fit for a king. We had been living in slums compared to this shit, but Bones knew, as I did, that we were on the come up.

We waited for Arnaudo by the poolside in comfortable lounging chairs. He didn't keep us waiting long, but he pretty much ignored Bones and walked up to me. He kissed my cheeks, then squeezed my hand with his. We walked off together to discuss business while Bones waited for us to get done. I saw him chatting away on his cell phone, and he kept looking at his watch. Arnaudo went on and on about some of his issues with Mango, but when all was said and done, he agreed to enter into a new contract with him. We shook on it, and before I left, he invited me to come back at a later day and time, without Bones. I promised him that I would.

The next stop was Carmen's place. As expected, she kept us waiting. We both were impatient, and by the time she came downstairs to meet with us, it was almost a quarter to one.

"I'm so sorry about the wait," she said. "I know the two of you want to get on the road, so I'll have Meecho get your package and take it to the car. Meanwhile, Mr. Bones, I want to show you around. Do you mind?"

In all of her elegance, she stood and reached out for his hand. Bones remained seated on the couch; then he stood up too. I assumed he was about to go somewhere and fuck the bitch, but as she moved, he halted her steps by pulling her hand toward him.

"Unfortunately, I'ma have to take a rain check. We need to get back on the road pronto. I'm not sure what delayed you, but I just don't have time to take the tour that you want me to. But I promise you that the next time

I come here, I will make time for you and only you. We can do whatever you want, and as a matter of fact, I'm looking forward to it."

Carmen appeared disappointed, but she also gazed at him with glee in her eyes. If I didn't know any better, I would've thought that bitch had fallen in love.

She reached out and touched the side of Bones's face. "When will you be coming back? Hopefully soon."

"I hope so too. Maybe within another week or two for sure."

"Okay," she said, then let go of his hand. "See you in a week or two then. Before then, please call me. I think it would be good to hear your voice sometimes."

"Sure," Bones said, then reached out to hug her. "We'll talk soon."

I wanted to throw the fuck up. But when Meecho put the package in the car and we drove off, I was relieved. This was another successful trip. Being with Bones wasn't so bad after all. He was a real nigga, and I teased him about having feelings for Carmen, even though he had previously denied it.

"She rubbed me the wrong way yesterday, but deep down, she seems like good people. I may tap into that pussy one of these days. Who knows what the future holds?"

"We don't know, but let me warn you about hooking up with her. She's a snake. And if you have sex with her, she's going to expect for you to move in with her. One of her husbands *supposedly* committed suicide, and another one has been missing for several years. You definitely don't want to mess with her head, and she ain't like these other ordinary chicks you be fucking with."

"Ain't nothing ordinary about the women I fuck with, so let's get that straight. And while you're over there preaching, you should be careful fucking with Arnaudo. His jealous ass don't seem to have it altogether either, so be careful messing with that dude."

"Please. What makes you think that I've hooked up with Arnaudo? It's all about business between us. Nothing more, nothing less."

"Feed that bullshit to somebody else. I know for a fact that he's had a piece of that pussy; the lustful look in his eyes said it all. I'm surprised that you hooked up with somebody like him though. He didn't seem like your type."

I pursed my lips and defended my actions. "Arnaudo is a very nice-looking man, so I don't know what you think my *type* is. And just for the record, I have never done anything with him. We keep it strictly business."

"If you say so, ma. Whatever you say I believe you."

Bones turned up the radio to tune me out. He wasn't buying what I was selling, and it wasn't long before I admitted to hooking up with Arnaudo *one* time.

"Just once," I said. "The sex was awful, and I promised myself that I would never go there again."

"What made the sex so awful? He didn't know how to utilize his tool or what?"

"No, he didn't, and he was too small. I like men with nice-sized packages and skillful moves. But unfortunately for me, it's been years since I've been blessed with a man like that. Maybe one of these days I'll get lucky again."

"Maybe so. But just so you know, I'm already taken. You'll never get lucky with me."

I playfully rolled my eyes at him. "That's good to know, but I'm not interested. You're not my type, and I have a serious problem with men who get thrills out of killing people."

"Well, there you have it. We're no match for each other, and you ain't interested in me, like I'm not interested in you. I hope we never have to revisit this conversation again, especially since we know where each other stands."

"True that," I said laying the seat back so I could take a nap. "Wake me when we get to Chicago."

BONES

I returned home to peace and quiet. Checked in with my grandmother to make sure she was good—she was. And after I met with Mango, and he upped my cash, I went home and slept on the floor like a newborn baby. The only time I left was to go get some food and stock the fridge. Other than that, I was happily stuck inside. I made a thick pallet on the floor, watched television, and ignored my phone. I finally checked my messages a few days later. Carmen called several times, and so did Alexis. Several text messages followed where she mentioned the results to the paternity test. Said we needed to talk. Soon. Mango left a few messages for me too. He wanted me to clear my schedule the weekend after next and travel to LA with Pebbles. That would be a long trip to take, so I had to mentally prepare myself for it. She was cool to be around, but she talked too damn much sometimes. Her attitude had slightly improved, and I somewhat liked how she got down when it came to business. She was very powerful in her own little way. But she still had a hot temper. I guess we both could learn a little something from each other, and that was always a good thing. I didn't mind letting her do things her way, but the only reason I intervened with her and the chief was because, well, I was turned the fuck on by her. It bothered me to watch him touching her, and I refused to stand there and watch her stroke his dick. I didn't know if she intended to suck it or not, but I wasn't about to watch that shit go down. That's why I ended it when I did. In no way would I tell her the real reason. She would think I was jealous and drive the shit out of me. Maybe even see it as a weakness in me. I definitely didn't want that.

Instead of calling Alexis back, I drove to her crib. I didn't want her to tell me anything over the phone, and I suspected that she had paperwork that revealed the results either way. I rang the doorbell. A few minutes later, she came to the door with Brianna standing a few feet behind her. There was no smile on Alexis's face when she let me in, and she immediately told Brianna to go in her room to play. Then she spoke to me.

"Have a seat in the living room, Bones. I'll be right back."

I went into the living room and sat on the arm of the couch. Alexis returned with two pieces of paper in her hand.

"Before I give you this, I want to tell you how sorry I am for putting everyone through this. Since Nate's death, I've had time to reflect on a lot of things. I have to take responsibility for some of the things I've done too, and a huge part of me regrets feeling the way I do about you. But I can't help it. These feelings are real, and I've never been able to hide them well."

She gave the paper to me, and when I opened it and saw that 99.9 percent I wasn't the father, I frowned. My face twisted, and I looked at Alexis with anger in my eyes.

"So, I guess you're trying to tell me now that Nate is Brianna's father, right?"

Alexis shook her head. "No, he isn't. There was someone else at the time, but he went to jail shortly after we hooked up. It has to be him, and I'm so sorry again for putting everybody through this. I just didn't know how much damage this would cause."

I shook my damn head, thinking about all that had happened. Women like Alexis made me fucking sick to my stomach. Her lies had done a lot of damage, and the main person who would feel the most pain from all of this would one day be Brianna. My face remained twisted as I tore up the letter and let the shreds fall to the floor.

"Now what, Alexis? Did you tell Brianna what happened to Nate?"

Her eyes watered as she looked at me. "No. I just told her he upped and left us. I don't want her to know the truth, even though she keeps asking about him."

"I don't know what to say about you right now. I could call you every name in the book, but it still won't do any good. You—"

She put up her hand to silence me. "I know, Bones, trust me, I know. And I hate that you're mad at me. I thought you would understand what I had been going through with Nate, but I guess you don't. You have no idea what he put me through, and I needed somebody to make me feel loved. That's why I turned to you."

"You didn't need to feel loved. All you wanted was some dick. Nate was out doing his thing, and yo' ass wanted revenge. Stop talking that love shit 'cause you know damn well that I wasn't representing like that."

Alexis lowered her head in shame. She wiped her tears, then swallowed a huge lump that appeared stuck in her throat. "What about us, Bones? Where do we go from here? Is this it, or is there any chance that we can now put all of this behind us for real and move on? I welcome your friendship, and there is no secret that I enjoy having sex with you. You may not have any love for me, but I like how you make me feel when we're together, with the exception of that one time. I know I've made some mistakes, but the question is, can you forgive me?"

I couldn't even respond to all of this soap opera bullshit she was swinging my way. And instead of saying anything else to her, I jetted. I drove off, thinking hard about her and Brianna. If Alexis didn't get her shit together, she guaranteed them a long and fucked-up road ahead. I damn sure didn't want that for Brianna, but my hands were tied right now.

I pressed on the brakes to stop at the red light. As I slowly turned my head to the left, I saw a car rush in beside me. Something didn't feel right about it, and the second I saw the window ease down, his eyes stared right into mine. A wicked grin washed across his face, causing me to duck and press hard on the accelerator. Bullets riddled my car. It spun in circles as tires screeched and burned rubber. I hurried to open the glove compartment and reached for my gun. Shattered glass from the broken windows covered me and cut my arms. I lay still until I heard a voice near my car.

"Is he dead?" I heard someone say. He peeked inside to check my status and got a personal introduction to my Glock. I fired three shots. One went into the nigga's forehead, and two went into his right eye. The other person in the car sped off, and before the scene got too chaotic, I got out of the car and ran. The car was one that Mango had given to me. It was registered in a dead man's name. My prints, however, were all over it. I guess this was one of those times when I needed Mango to cover for me.

I paced the floor in my loft while talking to him on the phone. He had already gotten several phone calls that confirmed the niggas who shot at me were cousins of Skittles. They did their homework to find out who I was and decided to come after me.

"I already got some people on this, but I want you to lie low around here for a while. Take a short trip if you have to. Go see Carmen or take an early trip to LA. Let me handle this one for you. These punks around here trying to be gangbangers, but they don't know who they fucking with. I'm glad you good, and I hope those cuts ain't nothing you can't handle."

I looked at the cuts on my arms. They were minor, but one was pretty deep. I kept applying pressure to it, hoping the bleeding would stop, especially since it was already wrapped.

"I'm fine. I got my arm wrapped, and it looks like the bleeding is slacking up."

"I don't want you to be fine. I want you to be at your best. I'ma send one of my special nurses over there to take a look at that cut. If need be, she'll take care of it for you. In the meantime, think about what I said. Let me know what you decide."

I told Mango that I would let him know. And after today, maybe I did need to go somewhere and chill. But not before I did what I felt was necessary. Nobody would take that many shots at me and get away with it. The license plate number of the muthafucka driving the car was locked in my brain. All I had to do was find out who he was and take care of things myself. I didn't want Mango to handle shit for me. And even though I trusted him, I still didn't trust the niggas who worked for him. They were all haters. They disliked me because they felt Mango gave me extraspecial treatment. So why in the hell would they have my back at a time like this? Hell no, they wouldn't.

The sweet little nurse that Mango told me he'd send to take care of me turned out to be Pebbles. When I opened the door, she smiled at me.

"I heard you done pissed off some people. And in the process, you got hurt. Let me take a look at your arms. That way, I can tell if you need me to work my magic on you or not."

Like always, Pebbles was dressed in all-black leather. A tight skirt and black, low-cut shirt that showed her cleavage. Her heels gave her much height, and as she came in from behind me, they clacked on the hardwood floors.

"I told Mango I was fine."

"That's not what he said."

She placed a small silver briefcase on the island, then asked to see my arms. As I stood in front of her, she removed the bandage to look at my cuts.

"This one needs stitches. The other cuts ain't as bad, but do you mind if I take care of that one for you?"

Without answering, I continued to hold out my arm. The cut was still oozing with blood. I watched as Pebbles put on some gloves and did her thing. I squeezed my eyes a few times from the needle going through my flesh, but minutes later I was all good.

"Thank you," I said. "Now if you don't mind, I need to go make some moves."

"Did Mango already send you a new car? I'm sure the other one you were driving ain't working anymore."

"He said another car was on the way and mentioned that it would be parked on the parking lot. I haven't been outside to see if it's there yet."

"Well, if it's not, I'll take you where you need to go. Where might that be?"

"To a furniture store," I lied. "As you can see, I need to go find some furniture to put in here."

"Sounds like fun. I have good taste too, so I can help."

My intentions were to go look for the nigga who shot at me earlier, but I figured I could go see what was up with that a little later. For now, I left with Pebbles. The car that Mango sent was there, but I let Pebbles drive, just in case someone was watching me. As she drove to the nearest furniture store, I kept looking in the mirrors and watching every car that drove by us. I guessed I was a little paranoid, and I had a damn good reason to be.

We arrived at the store minutes later. Pebbles helped me pick out a contemporary bedroom set and a set for the kitchen. Both were way above my budget, but I couldn't deny how dope they were. I set up delivery for the following day. After that, we stopped to get something to eat. That didn't take long because all Pebbles ate was a salad. She wasn't playing when it came to food. And I couldn't complain about a woman who cared enough about her temple to take care of it.

"Where to now?" she said, then yawned. "Do you need to go anywhere else?"

I laid the seat back, then sucked on a joint I had clipped between my fingers. "Yeah, I do need to go somewhere else, but I'm waiting for Mango to text me back some information before I go there."

I passed the joint to Pebbles, then checked my phone to see if Mango had hit me back. He hadn't, but Alexis had sent me a text. The only thing it said was: Sorry. I deleted it. I sent Mango a follow-up text, and within a few minutes he sent me a message:

No name yet, but spotted at bowling alley on Sixteenth Street. I told u we got u. Let us handle this.

My reply: No.

I asked Pebbles to take me to the bowling alley. And as soon as she drove on the parking lot, I spotted a gang of niggas standing next to the car from earlier. Music was blasting, a bunch of laughter and talking was going on, and no one appeared to be paying attention to their surroundings. Pebbles parked, then looked over at me.

"Are you getting ready to do what I think you gon' do?" she said.

"Yes. I'm going inside to bowl."

I reached for my Glock to check the bullets inside. It was fully loaded.

"Point out the fool who came after you and let me take care of this for you," Pebbles said. "All you gotta do is tell me which one so I don't make a mistake and hit some of those bitches over there who may just happen to be in the wrong place at the wrong time."

"See, that's where we differ. You're never in the wrong place at the wrong time. Socializing with the wrong mutha-fuckas always has consequences."

Pebbles laughed and agreed. I took a few more hits from the joint, then passed it back to her. "Stay here and don't get out of the car," I said.

"What if you get hurt? You know those niggas probably strapped too. Don't think for one minute that they ain't."

I held out my hand, knowing that Pebbles wouldn't listen to me and stay in the car. "Give me your gun. I may need it."

She cocked her head back and brushed me off. "Negro, please. Don't nobody use my shit but me. Now, if you need my assistance, I'll be more than willing to help."

Asking for her to have my back would put Pebbles in serious danger. But she loved to live on the edge like me. She got a thrill out of this shit, and I could see the excitement building in her eyes.

"Get out, stay close to me, and follow my lead."

I opened the car door, and so did she.

"Yeah, whatever. You need to stay close to me and hope that no one recognizes you."

Taking each other's advice, we stayed closed to each other. We cuddled as if we were a couple in love and had our faces turned toward each other as if we were in a deep conversation. As we neared the vehicle where several niggas stood, along with two females, I counted a total of seven people. There was no time to waste on conversation, and I was 100 percent sure that this was the car from earlier.

The driver was smoking a blunt while sitting down with the door open. Two niggas were next to him, and the others stood close by the trunk while talking to the females. As we got closer, I turned my head away from Pebbles and stared directly at the driver. His eyes were definitely familiar. He squinted at me, and in an instant, the smile on his face vanished. His face fell flat, and he nudged the nigga next to him. At that second, I knew that I had my man. I lifted my gun and moved quickly away from Pebbles. Fired off several shots that hit my target as he attempted to fall back on the seat and grab something. It was too late. Too late for him and too late for the muthafuckas who stood next to him. They were dead. Cooked. The others ran. Scattered like roaches and panicked when Pebbles fired bullets from her gun, making it sound like a war zone. It rained bullets, and people screamed, not knowing if they would be hit next.

"What the fuck!" one chick shouted as she tried to quickly unlock her car. Pebbles stood right next to her— gun pointed at her chest. "What's up with this? Do I know you?"

Pebbles shrugged. "Don't think so. But let me introduce myself."

She pulled the trigger, dropping the chick in an instant. Another nigga squirmed on the ground while crying out like a bitch for help. He was helped by a bullet in his back, compliments of Pebbles. She was fierce. Bold. And I liked that.

"Come on," I yelled to her. "Let's go!"

We ran toward the car, looking around and making sure the entire parking lot was clear. Dead bodies were everywhere. Blood flowed on the concrete, and I had to send a clear message to Skittles's sidekicks that I, Mr. Bones, wasn't to be fucked with. Not now. Not never.

Almost an hour later, we returned to my loft high as fuck. We had stopped to get a bottle of Henny, and as we sat on the floor in the living room tossing back alcohol, I moved closer to Pebbles.

"You know you sexy, don't you?" I slurred with a wide smile.

"Sexy and tipsy, yes, I know."

"We both are, so why don't we finish the night off with a wild-ass sex session then?"

Pebbles laughed, then sipped from the bottle. "Sex? With you? Nah, no thanks. I'll pass."

I licked my lips, then grabbed my dick, holding it. "Pass on this? Why would you pass on all of this?"

"'Cause you're not my type. I thought I already made that known to you."

I moved closer to wrap my arms around her. My lips touched her ear. "I know what you said, but I don't believe you. And if I'm not your type, I'm willing to do whatever to make you change your mind."

She pulled away from me, then stood up. "It's hard for me to change my mind, but thanks for allowing me to come over and take care of you. It's late, and I'm going home. I'll see you in a few days, and I hope you'll be ready to drive to LA. Until then, go take a cold shower and get some sleep. You need it."

Pebbles walked away, leaving me high and dry, and hard as fuck. She removed her purse and the briefcase from the island, then waved to me before leaving. I lay back on the floor and released a deep, disappointed sigh. The ceiling fan turned from above, making me real dizzy. My eyelids got heavy, but my dick wouldn't go down because I kept thinking about Pebbles. All I wanted to do was hit that pussy one time. Just once. That's all I needed. I couldn't recall the last time I wanted to feel the insides of a bitch so badly. I definitely wanted to feel and taste all of her.

My thoughts of Pebbles led me to a place I really didn't want to be. It was almost two in the morning when I knocked on Alexis's door. She opened the door in a silk pajama shirt that was cut right underneath her fat pussy. Her long, messy hair flowed past her shoulders, and her face was pretty, but pale. I could tell she had been asleep.

"Do you know what time it is?" she said in a groggy tone.

"I do. But I wanted to come over and tell you that I forgive you."

She shook her head, rejecting what I'd just said. "No, you don't, Bones. You hold grudges and seek revenge. I know that for a fact."

I shrugged, then moved closer to wrap my arms around her waist. With my body close to hers, I was sure she felt how hard I was. "I do hold grudges, but this time, I won't seek revenge. Take your clothes off and I'll prove it to you."

Alexis never denied me. She pulled the shirt over her head and stood naked. I moved her back to the couch and fucked her again, as if she was the last bitch on earth.

"Bones, you have to stop doing this to me," she whined as my dick busted her sweet cherry and made it bleed. I tackled her hard from behind, and with her hands squeezed in mine, she griped about me holding her fingers too tight.

"It feels as if you're about to break it. Loosen your grip and slow this shit down. My pussy can't take this. I want . . . *need* for you to make love to me."

I didn't know what the fuck making love to her meant, but I did honor her wishes by slowing things down a little. I backed out of her and let her ride me until she couldn't ride much more. But by nine o'clock that morning, it was a wrap. I was back at my loft in a deep sleep, lying naked on the floor.

I woke up hours later because somebody was knocking at my door. My gun was on the floor next to me, so I reached for it, then quietly made my way to the door. Through the peephole I saw a man from the furniture store with a uniform on. I figured he was there to deliver my furniture, so I hurried to put on my robe, then opened the door.

"I have a delivery for uh, Bones. Is that you?"

"He ain't here, but he told me to be here when his furniture arrived."

"Okay," he said, handing me a clipboard with a piece of paper clipped to it. "Sign here."

I signed a bogus name on the paper. The man said he would be back with the furniture. He came back with two other men who assembled my bedroom furniture, along with the kitchen set. Everything was on point. The only other things left for me to pick out were some living room furniture and pictures for the bare walls. Curtains would murder the huge picture windows, so I intended to leave them as is.

After the men left, I lay across the bed, then reached for my phone. I called Pebbles to thank her again for helping me yesterday.

"No problem," she said. "I told you I had good taste."

"I can't agree with you on that, especially since you didn't take me up on my offer last night. But it's all good. I picked up my face after you left, and I'll never make the mistake of letting it get cracked again."

"Don't. It wasn't a pretty sight, and I felt horrible for you. It almost looked as if you wanted to cry, but I'm sure that one of your bitches was willing and able to wipe those tears for you, and then some."

"It's a good thing that you're starting to know me well. But on another note, I spoke to Mango this morning. He thinks we should head to LA today. I'm game if you are, but we have to make a stop in Atlanta first. Big L wants to give us something to take to Jake. And it's good business if I keep my word and stop by Carmen's place for the *tour* she wants to give me."

"You know damn well she doesn't want to give you a tour. She wants to fuck your brains out. Are you planning to go there with her?"

"Nope. She likes to flirt, and so do I. Mango thinks it's a good thing for me to stay on her good side, considering what she's worth. I agree."

"I don't, but do you, and I'ma do me. What time shall I meet you?"

"Come by at one. I should be ready by then."

Feeling real energized today, I cleaned up well and rocked a pair of black slacks and a button-down royal-blue shirt with suspenders. The shirt tightened on my muscular frame, and my cologne had a bite to it. Not only did I feel good, but I looked good too and smelled like millions. Pebbles called to tell me that she was waiting for me on the parking lot. I went downstairs and saw her parked between two cars. Her eyes were glued to me. Her mouth looked stuck open—she appeared to be in a trance, *hooked* more like it, but she was trying to play hard to get. I didn't mind. I figured that one day she would be in the same place as Alexis was.

Pebbles got out of the car wearing black stretch leggings. A black leather jacket covered her black wife beater, and her black heels had silver studs on them. She must've been allergic to color. I wondered if she ever wore anything else, but I didn't ask because I didn't want her to think that my comment was an insult. Commenting also meant I was paying attention to her. I didn't want her to know that I was.

"Look at you," she said with a smile. "I wonder who you're trying to impress. Would that be Carmen?"

I ignored Pebbles. She followed behind me as I made my way to the car. We both got inside, and then I drove off.

"I don't appreciate you ignoring me all the time, and please don't get mad when I start ignoring you," she said.

"In case you haven't noticed, I don't get mad."

"Right. You get even."

She was starting to know me all too well. I drove to a nearby gas station to fill the tank. To my surprise, when I exited, I ran into Alexis and Brianna. They were on their way inside and had just walked past the car I was in. Brianna ran up to me and gave me a hug. I lifted her in my arms, really happy to see her.

"Hi, Mr. Bones," she said. "I'm glad to see you, but, uh, have you seen my dad? And why don't you stop by to see us as much as you used to?"

I glanced at Alexis who had turned her head to look in another direction.

"Because I got a new job that's been keeping me real busy. I haven't seen Nate, but as soon as I do, I'll be sure to tell him to call you or stop by. He's probably real busy too. And I bet that he's missing you too."

Brianna smiled. She was a happy little girl, considering all of the bullshit that had been going on around her. After I put her down, she rushed over to Alexis and took her hand.

"Mommy, I want some candy. Will you buy me some M&Ms?"

"Yes. As soon as I go inside to pay for the gas."

I reached in my pocket and gave Brianna a ten-dollar bill. "Get your M&Ms and some gummy bears. You like those too, don't you?"

She nodded, then took the money from my hand.

"What do you say?" Alexis said.

"Thank you, Mr. Bones. Thank you very much."

"You're welcome."

Alexis looked me up and down, then smiled. "I love the fit you rocking. Where are you on your way to?"

"To take care of something for a friend."

"Will you have time to stop by later? I can cook dinner for you, if you'd like."

"Thanks, but I won't have time. We'll hook up some-time next week."

Alexis accepted what I said, then she went inside to pay for her gas. I saw Pebbles watching us the entire time. I hurried to pump the gas so we could go. But just as I hit the thirty-dollar mark, Alexis came out of the gas station and walked my way with Brianna holding her candy. Alexis's eyes shifted from Pebbles to me.

"Why didn't you introduce me to your friend?" she said. "Then again, I didn't know you had any more friends."

"I don't."

"Really? Then, if you don't mind me asking, who is she?"

"I do mind," I said as I was done pumping gas.

Alexis boldly walked to the passenger's side and tapped on the window. Pebbles lowered it with attitude written on her face.

"Hi," Alexis said. "I'm a close friend of Bones. I don't think we've met before, have we?"

"We haven't, but I'm a close friend too. I guess Bones is good at keeping his friends a secret."

"Yeah, I am." I got in the car, then closed the door. I looked at Alexis who was still bent over and staring into the car. "Like I said, we'll holla soon. Until then, take care of Brianna and make sure she get some more of those M&Ms."

Alexis rolled her eyes, then told me to wait. She came to my side of the car. I lowered the window, and she bent over again.

"I wanted to let you know that Nichelle is bugging me about talking to you about Theo. I barely have time to get at you myself, and every time you come over, like you did last night, you're always in and out, if you know what I mean. Either way, she asked if I would give her your number. I don't know if you want me to do that or not."

"No. I don't have anything to say to her. If she wants answers about what Theo did, she needs to revisit some of the shit that was on his mind at the time or get at the police."

"Okay. I'll tell her that. Be safe and we'll talk later."

Alexis leaned in to plant a kiss on my lips. Normally, I wouldn't reciprocate, but this time I pecked her lips back.

"Bye, Bones," she said then walked away with Brianna.

I raised the window, then shifted in my seat to look at Pebbles who had her lips pursed. "You know, some tricks be acting real silly and thirsty. She just *had* to let me know that you were with her last night. I'm so glad that . . ." She paused. "Never mind."

"Naw, go ahead and speak your mind. What were you about to say?"

"Nothing. Other than I will never let you put your dick inside of me. I have a feeling that you got some of that potent shit that can make a bitch go crazy. That heifer was a prime example. She didn't have to come over here and say anything to me. It's apparent that you don't give two cents about her. And the only reason you probably still dealing is because of your daughter. She's cute. They're both cute, but your daughter looks just like you."

Her comment caught me a little off guard, but I didn't elaborate on the real deal. It wasn't her business.

"I'm sure Alexis would disagree with your assessment of her."

"Usually I'm right."

I saved that discussion for another day. We had a long drive ahead of us, and by the time we made it to Atlanta, Pebbles had gone to sleep. I awakened her when we arrived at Carmen's place. Carmen stood at the door looking like a dolled up Jennifer Lopez. The sheer and breezy dress she rocked wasn't hiding nothing. Pebbles didn't care to see her goodies, so she rolled her eyes.

"If you go in there and fuck her, I will never stop dissing you. Besides, we don't have much time to waste. I want you to meet some interesting people in LA. Family included. They are going to help us in a major way, so we need to wrap up our business here and get back on the road."

"Promise I won't be long. She only wants to give us a tour."

"She didn't mention giving *us* a tour, only *you*. The farthest I've ever gotten in her house is to the living room. I told you before that me and this bitch don't click."

"Maybe not but money talks, bullshit walks. Leave it in the car and let's get this over with."

Pebbles followed me as I got out of the car and walked up the concrete stairs to the porch with large white columns. Carmen was all smiles. She threw her arms around my neck, expressing how happy she was to see me again.

"I've been thinking a lot about you," she said. "We haven't had an opportunity to talk, but I assume that you've been very busy."

"You ain't said nothing but a word. Very busy, and then some."

She released me. We walked inside together. A butler stood in the foyer, waiting for Carmen to give him direction.

"Pebbles, I want you to go with Clarence. He fixed you something so amazing in the kitchen. I'm sure you're going to love it. I need to speak to Bones in private about something imperative. I'm sure you understand."

Pebbles looked at me, then released a deep sigh. Much attitude was on display, but she followed Clarence as he led the way toward the kitchen. Carmen and I headed upstairs. The double staircase was covered with a rich burgundy carpet. The long hallway was too, and many exquisite paintings covered the walls. Double glass doors could be seen at the end of the hall. When we entered the master suite, it was off the chain. A huge bed sat in the center of a marble-topped floor. Long drapes covered the double bay windows, and an entertainment center stretched from one wall to the next. A fireplace made of marble sat to the left, and two chaises were in front of it. Carmen sat on one of the chaises, then invited me to have a seat on the other one. She popped the cap on a bottle of champagne, and then poured it in two flute glasses, handing me one.

"Thanks," I said, still looking around at the dope-ass room. "You got a nice-ass crib."

"Yes, I do. And if you play your cards right, you can have a place like this too. I'll get straight to the point and tell you why I wanted to meet with you in private. Mango is scum. You can do better than him. I want you to come here and work for me. I can use a man with your talents, skills, charisma, and charm. Also, with your good looks. I will pay you double what Mango is paying you. And trust me when I say his money will never match mine."

I was shocked by her offer and by her feelings about Mango. Thing is, I didn't know if this was a setup or not. This could have easily been planned, just to see what direction I would move in. So for now, I pretended I wasn't interested, even though I was.

"I appreciate the offer, but if you don't mind me saying, loyalty means everything to me. I have no complaints with Mango, and he takes good care of me. I could never see giving up my gig with him and coming to work for you."

Carmen side-eyed me while sipping from her glass. She placed it on the table, then crossed her long legs. The sheer dress she had on had a sexy slit on the side. It slid over and revealed her silky smooth thighs that were tanned and toned, like the rest of her body.

"I'm going to allow you some time to think about my offer. It will stay on the table for now, but not for long. All I ask is that you give it some serious thought and let me know."

"Will do. Thanks for your understanding, and again, the offer is much appreciated."

Carmen smiled. She then stood and walked over to me. She got on her knees in front of me, then took the glass from my hand.

"Now that we took care of that, let's move on to the next order of business."

I said not one word as she unlatched my black leather belt, pulling it from around my waist. She unzipped my pants, and when I stood, she eased them down to my ankles, along with my Calvin Klein briefs. My hard dick damn near slapped her in the face as she held it tight. She looked it over, then sucked the whole thing into her warm mouth. I pumped hard while holding her head and moving it to the rhythm of my strokes. She sucked me so good—as if she was sucking my skin off. I couldn't believe how hard and horny I was. Unfortunately, though, I had to cut her short and move on to other things. I lifted her from the floor, then straddled her around my waist. After stepping out of my pants, I carried her over to the bed, laying her on the soft silk white comforter. I parted her legs, then reached for her pink lace panties that showed her fat pussy. The sweet aroma from her pussy made me high. I needed something new. Something different. Something more satisfying. She presented herself to be exactly what I was looking for. Her legs trembled from my touch. I could tell she was a little nervous, but when I put on a condom and hit her with a gentle stroke, her trembles ceased. She wrapped her legs around my back and kept at a slow pace with me as I slid in and out of her moist hole. Her firm breasts wobbled around, and as I leaned forward to get a mouthful of them, she grabbed the back of my neck.

"I had a feeling that you would feel this good inside of me," she whispered. "Is this why they refer to you as Mr. Bones? Your bone feels like one in a million."

I was glad that she thought so, especially since I hadn't given her my all yet. Maybe one day I would, but today I held back a little. My mind was focused on the offer she had made me. Was there a chance for something like that to work out? Would Mango be down with me moving on and be willing to set me free, without any bullshit? I didn't think so, but I always knew how to get over hurdles. Been jumping over them all of my life. Maybe it was time for me to jump higher.

Carmen's moans and groans echoed loudly in the room. I was so sure that somewhere behind all of the mirrors on the wall, we were being either watched or taped. I didn't have shit to hide, so I stepped up my game and gave Carmen some more action. My thick fingers entered her pussy, and I used my thumb to tickle her clit. My dick tackled both holes, and she rode the shit out of me during anal sex. She was highly experienced, and she handled my strokes like a pro. I soon resumed in her sopping wet pussy that had cream boiling over it like hot lava. This was no virginlike pussy she was serving me, and she was all woman. My length let her know I was all man. My steel was far up in her, causing her whimpers to turn into loud cries. Her pussy thumped fast, and that's when another orgasm erupted. She pulled at her hair, then snatched my hand away from her swollen pearl.

"Nooooo," she hollered out. "I mean, yes yes yes! Fuck me some more! Give meeeeee more, Bones, mooooore!"

I honored her request, but within the hour, we wrapped it up in the spacious shower with waterfall faucets. Water sprayed our naked bodies all over, and after I finished bending her over the seat while fucking her brains out, she'd finally had enough. She looked beat, but I looked and felt fresh as ever. I put my clothes back on, and once Carmen slid into a silk robe, we returned to the lower level. Pebbles and Clarence were hollering at each other in the kitchen when we walked in. A tray with shrimp cocktail, seafood dip, and crabmeat was on the table. So was another tray with an array of fruits. I was sure that Pebbles appreciated Carmen's generosity. Then again, by the look on her face . . . maybe not.

"I see the two of you have been enjoying yourselves," Carmen said to Pebbles.

She didn't respond. She narrowed her eyes and looked at me with a mean mug locked on her face. Carmen, however, had a look as if she'd just been fucked—well. Nothing could wash the smile off her face.

"Did I say or do something wrong?" she asked Pebbles.

"No," Pebbles said, then looked at her watch. "But we need to go. We're running way behind schedule, and people don't like it when we're late."

"I understand and most definitely agree." She looked at me. I picked up an apple and bit into it. She touched the side of my face, then shot me a wink. "Don't forget to give much thought to what I said, handsome. And this time, I look forward to hearing from you sooner."

She left the kitchen, and we followed behind her. Pebbles barely looked my way, but I didn't trip off her attitude. The only thing it was going to get her was left behind.

Pebbles

I couldn't believe that Bones had fucked that nasty bitch Carmen. I don't know why I assumed he wouldn't, but I now knew that he wasn't all about business as he pretended to be. He was doing the ho thing too. That disappointed me. Disturbed me to the point where I didn't have much else to say to him right now. I was ready to take care of this little situation with Big L, then get to LA, where I had plenty of family and friends. My plan was to leave Bones and let him drive back by himself. Being in his presence wasn't where I wanted to be. I hated that he'd made me feel this way—it had been a long time before any nigga tampered with my feelings. I was jealous. And it wasn't a good thing for a woman who was as confident and sure of herself as I was to show my weakness, especially in front of another woman. I didn't like it. He made me feel that since I wouldn't give up the pussy last night, the next bitch was just as good as me. The glee in Carmen's eyes made me ill. She hated my guts, and she knew that fucking Bones would mess with my head. Bad. I regretted my reaction, but I couldn't ignore the numerous suck marks on her neck and breasts. Her wet hair and change of clothes let me know they must have showered together. She looked overly satisfied, but the look on Bones's face I couldn't read. He was always so nonchalant. Serious. Very cold too. I wanted to ask him why he lied to me about not wanting to have sex with her, but I decided against it. It wasn't my business. He wasn't my man, and I was sure that he never would be.

Bones pulled in a parking spot at Big L's place, then shifted the car in park. I sat there, still quiet as a mouse.

"You don't need to come inside unless you want to," he said. "All Mango told me to do is pick up a package. That shouldn't take long."

"I hope not because we need to get back on the road. Tell Big L I said what's up. Hurry back and bring me back a joint. I need something to smoke."

He nodded, then got out of the car. I watched as he checked his surroundings and smooth walked toward the apartment complex to go up the stairs. As soon as I saw him go inside, his phone vibrated. I picked it up to look at who was calling. On the screen was a naked picture of Carmen with her legs wide open. The text message she sent said: I'm already eager to feel you again. Hope you can make it back this way soon.

I started to send that bitch a fucked-up message, but instead, I deleted her text and picture. I flipped through some of his other pictures, shaking my head at the numerous trifling bitches who wanted to show him what they could serve him. One chick had her pussy so close to the camera that he could damn near taste it. I was appalled, so I tossed the phone on the seat and rolled my eyes. I waited impatiently for Bones to return, until I had to pee. My legs were held tightly together, so I exited the car to go look for a restroom near the park area. The one that was there was locked, so I headed toward the car. I didn't feel like climbing several stairs to Big L's apartment, but before making it back to the car, I didn't have a choice.

I turned to go up the stairs, but halted my steps when I saw Big L's right-hand man, Keith, pull his car beside ours. He was on his cell phone, looking highly suspicious. I wasn't sure what was up, so I put my piss on hold and walked toward his car. He lowered the window to speak to me.

"Damn, you too fine to have that mean look on yo' face. And I know you'd better speak."

This nigga knew I didn't have no love for him, so my tone was dry. "What's up? I didn't recognize you."

"Sure you didn't. But, uh, what you doing here?"

"I'm waiting on Bones. He went inside to pick up something from Big L. I'm surprised you didn't know we would be stopping by."

"He told me, but I had several runs to make. You know that nigga Big L always got me on missions and shit."

I put my hands in my pockets, then leaned against Bones's car. "What's the word on those white bitches and the chief? I know people been talking around here, haven't they?"

"That shit has been on the news almost every day. But you already know how it goes around here. Ain't nobody seen or heard nothing. You and Bones did good."

Speaking of Bones, I wondered what was taking him so long. I turned to reach for his phone inside of the car so I could call Big L. As I bent over, Keith reached out to grab my ass. I swung around displaying a frown and snapped on his ass.

"Don't touch me, nigga. Shit like that will get you fucked up."

"Bitch, please. You know you like it. Stop acting like you don't."

"I just told you I didn't like it. Do you need me to confirm it?"

He laughed, then reached out again. This time, he squeezed my right breast and tried to pinch my nipple. I slapped his hand away from my breast and quickly reached for my Glock that was tucked behind me. I aimed it at his face, but all he did was release a cackling laugh.

"Calm down, bitch, and stop trying to act all tough and shit. All I did was pull on those tiny titties to help them grow."

Insulting me was only going to get this nigga dead. I didn't hesitate to pull the trigger. The gun jerked me backward, and I watched a bullet pierce the air and go right into the side of his fat, greasy neck. His eyes bugged. He gasped out loudly, then reached up to squeeze his neck. Blood seeped through his fingers, and as he attempted to speak, it sounded like his ass was gargling water. I shoved his ass to the side, causing him to fall over on the seat.

Checking my surroundings, I saw one dude with several trash bags in his hand walking to a Dumpster. He kept his eyes focused on me, so I eased into Bones's car and slumped down. I tapped my feet, hoping that he hurried the fuck up, especially when I saw the dude reaching for his cell phone. I thought about getting out of the car to lullaby his ass, but as I placed my hand on the door handle, I saw Bones coming down the stairs. He had a brown paper bag in his hand, and when he looked at the dude by the trash can, he tossed his head back. Bones put the package in the trunk, then got in the car, and shut the door. He looked over at me, immediately asking what was wrong. I wasn't sure if I should tell him that I had just murdered Keith or not. But my mind was made up when I thought about the consequences.

"Nothing," I rushed to say. "Let's just go. I want to get away from here."

Bones sped away, and as soon as we hit the highway his cell phone vibrated. He said that it was Mango, then answered.

"What up?" Bones paused. His face got tight, and he gazed ahead without a blink. "What?" he yelled. "Hell, nah, man. She's with me, so I know it didn't go down like that. Them niggas tripping."

He paused again, but this time he shifted to look at me. I bit my lip, then turned my head to look out of the window.

"Hold," Bones said, then gave the phone to me. "Here. Take it."

I put the phone up to my ear. "Yes."

"Yes, my ass!" Mango yelled. "Bitch, please tell me that you didn't just do anything that stupid! Did you shoot that nigga Keith?"

At first, I was going to lie, but since that muthafucka by the trash can had already snitched on me, I had to fess up. I knew I should've gotten out of the car to smoke his ass. Big mistake.

"Yes, I did. He groped me while I stood by his car, then called me a bunch of bitches and hoes. I didn't appreciate that shit, Mango. Don't no nigga diss me like that, and you already know how I am."

There was a crisp silence, but then I heard Mango breathing heavily into the phone. He cleared his throat, and then yelled into the phone. "You are a bitch, Pebbles. As well as a dumb ho! You done fucked up, baby. Done fucked up real bad. Big L wants yo' ass dealt with, and I don't blame him. Brang yo' ass back here right now, so we can discuss how to stop the muthafuckin' bleeding!"

The phone went dead. I guess that sucker was mad. He was sadly mistaken if he thought I was going to come back right now and talk. Talk, my ass. Mango was pissed, and I was sure that he had something real wicked in store for me.

"Please tell me you didn't do it," Bones said calmly.

I caught an attitude because I didn't understand why they thought it was okay for that grimy nigga to put his hands on me and for me not to do anything.

"I did it, and I'm glad I did. Keith had that shit coming. I told you before that I was gon' get that ass, didn't I?"

Bones got off the highway to slow down.

"Why are you slowing down? What's up?"

He pulled over to the curb, then put the car in park. As he looked at me, his eyes showed much seriousness. "I don't think you understand the severity of what you just did. And I'm not saying that it's okay for any muthafucka to touch you or call you names. But when it comes to business, you have to choose your battles carefully, or else you'll lose. That wasn't a battle you were going to win. Bottom line, you fucked up. You should've waited and told me or Mango how Keith disrespected you. We could have notified Big L and let him handle that fool."

I waved him off. "Bones, please. You and Mango wouldn't have done shit about it. I chose my battle carefully, and that nigga needed to die. I don't care who disagrees with me on this, but too damn bad." I looked straight-ahead, then crossed my arms in front of me with much attitude. "Now, let's roll. I have places to go and other people to see."

Bones shook his head. He squeezed his forehead with the tips of his fingers, then cracked his knuckles. I could tell he was in deep thought. We sat in silence for a few minutes, and when his phone vibrated, he answered. Instantly, I could hear Mango yelling through the phone.

"Do not go to LA! Brang that bitch back to me now!"

Bones sighed, then shut his eyes. "We on our way," he said, then hit the end button.

"I'm not going back there with you," I said. "Take me to LA."

He snapped his head to the side, giving me a hard stare. "This ain't no goddamn game, Pebbles. Wake the fuck up! I can't take you to LA, and if you think they won't turn you over to Big L or Mango, you are fooling your damn self."

"My peoples won't do that. I got some loyal connections there who don't give a fuck about Mango. They got my back, and after the dust settles, then I'll deal with Big

L and Mango. Not now, though. Everybody hot about what happened, but one day they'll understand where the fuck I was coming from."

"It'll be a cold day in hell when they do. You are living in fantasyland if you think this is going to smooth over. I don't know what else to say to you, but I need to go somewhere, chill, and get my mind right. I can't see myself taking you back to Mango, nor am I driving you to LA. I need to think about some other options."

I already knew what I was going to do. That was get the fuck out of Dodge and get to LA as quickly as I could. But since it was late, I remained in the car with Bones and stayed with him as he got a room for us at a hotel. His phone had been ringing off the hook, but he didn't answer. I hated to put him in the middle of this shit, but that muthafucka Keith shouldn't have ever touched me.

Bones sat on the couch with his hands clenched together. A cigar dangled from his mouth, and his foot kept tapping the floor. He was in deep thought, just as I was as I sat in a chair across from him.

"Don't go to LA," he said. "If you go there, you die."

"And if I go back to Chicago, I die. You already know that Mango will do some serious harm to me. I don't really have a choice. Besides, I have family in LA. I need to get there soon. If you don't take me, I'll get there the best way I can."

Bones laid his head back on the couch. "I'm not taking you there. I think you should go somewhere else and chill for a while. I'll tell Mango that you hopped out of the car at a gas station and ran off. All you need to do is figure out where else you can go, other than LA."

Where I intended to go wasn't for him to decide. But I told him I would think about another place, even though LA was my next destination. He didn't say anything else to me. Was real quiet and pondering like a muthafucka.

A few minutes later, he picked up the phone and walked into the other room. I listened in. I heard him tell Mango that we were on our way back, after he got a few hours of rest. I wasn't sure what Mango said, but Bones didn't reply. He sat on the bed, and that's when I went into the room where he was.

"I appreciate your help, and by morning, I'll decide if LA is in my plans or not. Regardless, I'll let you know."

Bones shrugged. I could tell he was highly upset with me, but deep down, he had no idea how afraid and confused I really was. He picked up the remote to turn on the TV. I left him at peace and went to think this shit out on the couch.

A few hours later, I woke up, realizing that I had slept too long. Thank God for the loud thumping in the other room. I could hear somebody fucking. The headboard was banging against the wall, and her moans let me know that the dick inside of her was pretty damn good. I glanced at the alarm clock. It showed five minutes after three in the morning. I got up and tiptoed toward the bedroom. Bones was lying on the bed knocked the fuck out. I could hear him snoring. My eyes shifted to the keys on the nightstand, and I thought about my plan from earlier—taking the keys and driving to LA myself. That appeared to be the best thing for me, so I moved further into the room, hoping not to wake Bones.

While holding my breath, I went for the keys. But as soon as I had my hand on them, Bones reached out and grabbed my hand. He squeezed it tight. Looked at me as if he could kill me.

"What in the fuck are you doing?" he barked.

"I . . . I was going to the car to get something. I didn't want to wake you."

He released my hand, then jumped up from the bed and stood directly in front of me. With my high heels on, I was only a few inches shorter than him.

"Don't play me like I'm a goddamn fool," he hissed. "Yo' ass was about to flee. Tell me this, how fucking stupid are you? I thought you had a bit more sense than this, but I'm starting to think that I was dead wrong about you."

I swallowed the lump in my throat, then backed a few inches away from him. "You can think what you want, Bones. I was just going to the car to get something."

He caught me completely off guard when he grabbed my neck and used all of his strength to push me away from him. I tumbled over the bed and hit the floor so hard that it felt as if my back had cracked. My brows arched inward as I hurried off the floor and charged toward him. I was met by his tight grip again. He squeezed my neck, then backed me up to the wall, slamming my head against it. I felt dizzy as fuck. Sore all over, and as he lifted me from the ground, my feet dangled. I was in so much pain. Couldn't breathe, couldn't talk. Tears began to seep from my eyes, and that's when he let me go. I dropped to the floor, coughing and trying to catch my breath.

"Charge at me again," he said, "and your life ends today."

He didn't have to worry about me charging him again. I continued to cough and did my best to catch my breath. My whole body ached, so I crawled on the floor until I was able to stand. I could barely stand, so I moved over to the bed and plopped down. I wiped my watery eyes, then looked at the evilness staring back at me.

"I'm sorry, okay?" I said, then coughed again. "I just didn't know what to do. I figured I could leave now, and no one would ever find me. I didn't trust you not to tell Mango my whereabouts. If you drop me off somewhere, I'm sure you're going to tell him."

"I don't trust yo' ass either, but if I was going to turn you over to Mango or tell him your whereabouts, I would have done so by now. I don't like to be played like a fucking fool, and being around slick-ass women don't work for me."

"I wasn't trying to betray you. I was just doing what I thought would be best for me. I don't know how I'm going to get out of this mess, and the last thing I want . . ." I paused, thinking about the shit and finally realizing just how bad this was. "I'm not ready to die. We both know that Mango is going to kill me. Big L will have it no other way, and he's probably asking, right now, that my head be delivered to him on a silver platter."

Tears started to fall from my eyes, but I hurried to smack them away. I hated to be emotional around people, especially men. That's why I played the tough role all the time. I hid my feelings well, but in this moment, and at this time, I couldn't hold back. This was deep.

I shielded my face with my hands, then wiped down it. I looked at Bones who stood with an unsympathetic, cold look on his face.

"What am I going to do?" I cried out. "Don't look at me like that, and you've got to understand why I did what I did. I don't have all of the answers right now, but go ahead and tell me what you think I should do. Mainly, where should I go."

At first, he didn't say anything. Just stared as if he was trying his best to read me. I was in a lot of pain. Confused and ready to listen to whatever his suggestion was.

"Bones, please say something. I'll listen to whatever you say. I don't have no other choice, and time is not on my side."

He finally spoke up. "Stop all that fucking crying right now 'cause it ain't gon' do you no damn good. You should've thought about that shit earlier when I told you this shit was serious. Too bad you had to sleep on it to realize how bad things really are. I had some other ideas swarming in my head, but now I think it's best for you to take the car. Take it and go to any other place than LA. I don't even want to know where you're going. I'll tell Mango that you stole the car while I was asleep. The money from Big L is still in the trunk so use it. Ditch the car as soon as you can and disappear. Don't call me—don't call no one."

I blinked fast to fight back my tears, but this was too much. What did he mean by disappear? I didn't want to be somewhere in another country, all by my damn self and with no one to turn to. No one to talk to—just living. I put my hands over my face and started to cry harder. He was right. . . . This *was* fucked up. I had fucked up. And even though I didn't want to go into hiding, I came to the conclusion that it was best. All I could think of was what kind of life would I have, always being on the run, watching my back and not knowing if Mango or Big L would ever catch up with me. Nonetheless, I had to go. Had to do something. I didn't want Bones in the middle of this, and this was the best way out for both of us. Mango would give Bones hell about me fleeing, no doubt, but I was sure that Bones could handle the situation and say the right thing.

I had hyped myself up to go, but I couldn't get my shit together. I was sure that Bones was calling me all kinds of weak, stupid bitches in his head. I sobbed like a baby, but I kept my hands over my face so he wouldn't see my eyes. I was shocked when I felt him sit on the bed next to me. His arm went around my shoulders, and he pulled me close to his chest.

"It's gon' be all right," he said in a whisper. "Stop crying and go do what you gotta do. You got that fight in you, girl. That bite. Something like this can't stop you from surviving."

His words provided just a little comfort. And sitting here crying wasn't going to do me any good. I pulled away from his chest, then cleared my wet face with my hands. Bones handed me the keys, and I took a deep breath before standing up. My legs felt weak, and my back was still aching from when he'd tossed me on the floor. A headache was trying to come too.

"I guess I'll see you when I see you," I said, reaching for my purse. "And how are you going to get back to Chicago?"

"Don't worry about it. I'll get there. Just go. Now."

I made my way to the door, but quickly turned around to give Bones one last look, just in case I would never see him again. I loved the way I felt when I looked at him. Protected. The same way my father made me feel . . . before he was killed. I was eleven years old, and watched in a closet as he was murdered right in front of me. He was my rock. My everything. The only man I had ever looked up to and loved dearly. Bones had a lot in common with my father. He was, without a doubt, the kind of man I had waited a lifetime to find. Unfortunately for me, my timing was off.

"Go," he said with a frown on his face while cocking his head to the side.

"I will. But I need to take care of one last thing."

I rushed up to him, then leaned in to kiss him as he sat on the bed. At first, he wouldn't open his mouth. I forced my tongue between his lips, and shortly thereafter, he opened his mouth wide. My tongue went further inside to dance with his. Juicy. Wet. Stimulating and pleasurable. So intense that I forced him back on the bed and lay on top of him. He secured his arms around my waist, then lowered his hands to massage my ass. I wanted him so badly. Needed to feel him inside of me. Wanted to feel his dick sliding down my throat and also offer him a taste of my sweet, wet pussy. But Bones stopped me. He pushed me away from him, then sat up.

"No," he said. "I'm not doing this with you."

"Why? Just let—"

"No!" he growled. He yelled so loud that I jumped.

"Okay," I said in a calm tone. "I'll go."

Bones lay back on the bed. He placed his hands behind his head, stared at the ceiling for a few minutes, then closed his eyes. I wanted to say something else to him, but I figured I would set him off. I walked to the door again. This time when I turned around, he was still on the bed with his eyes closed. I wiped another tear that had fallen, and then made my exit.

I kept driving until I couldn't drive anymore. My eyes were tired from crying so much. I couldn't even think straight. Bones advised me not to go to LA, but the truth of the matter was, I really had no other place to go. My cousin Sabrina would help me. I trusted her. She would make sure I had a safe place to hide. With that in mind, I filled my body with caffeine, put more gas in the tank, and against Bones's wishes, I headed to LA.

BONES

When I returned to Chicago, alone, Mango was acting a goddamn fool. His money was gone, and so was his car. Not to mention Pebbles.

"I'ma find that bitch if it's the last thing I do," he yelled, then slammed his hand on the table. "How dare her do some shit like this? Do you know all that I've done for that cock-sucking ho? I wish she was right here so I could beat her ass and break her fucking neck!"

I sat at the table listening and not saying a word. Yes, Pebbles had fucked up, but Keith shouldn't have gone there with her. Did he deserve to die? In my book, no. But Pebbles had a temper that she couldn't control. I was sure that her past had a lot to do with it, but I really didn't know much about her. All I knew was, I had some feelings for her. Nothing serious, no love, but there was something there. Something that I wanted more of, but now, it looked as if I would never know what that was.

"I gotta pay for that nigga's funeral, send his family some money, and send Jake his money in LA 'cause that trick stole it. Why in the fuck did you let her steal his money?"

I remained calm. I didn't get down like that with niggas like Mango. Raising my voice would set off a firestorm in here, so I was careful not to push the wrong buttons.

"I didn't think she would roll like that. Since you were the one who introduced me to her, I thought she was someone I could trust to a certain extent. I must say that

I'm disappointed myself, but if you mad at anybody, I think you may need to take a look in the mirror. You're the one who kept sending her out there, knowing that she was a hothead. She was trigger-happy, and she didn't know how to think before she acted. I'm sure that was something you've known about her for quite some time. Unfortunately, I didn't know, until the shit hit the fan. So what I'm basically saying is, this ain't on me."

Boom. I threw that shit back on Mango. He didn't have nothing to say. All he did was grunt and continue to rant about how much money he was going to lose, and how badly Pebbles had damaged his reputation. That only meant he'd send me on more missions to help repair the damage.

"I don't have no problem with helping to repair the damage, but let's allow things to settle down for a while. In a few more weeks, I'll hit the road and see if I can mend some fences. If not, so be it. We'll just keep doing what we do and see what more we can do to open some other doors. Big L and Jake ain't the only elite niggas in the game."

Mango nodded, then lightened the mean mug on his face. As he poured a drink, I cracked my knuckles.

"I wanted to mention something else to you too," I said, trying to change the subject and get his mind elsewhere, just in case he doubted my loyalty. "Carmen offered me a job. Asked me to work for her. I turned her down, but I just thought that was something you might want to know."

The room was soaked with silence. I wasn't sure if that was the right move or not, but I didn't want him to suspect any wrongdoings with me and Pebbles. There was also a chance that Mango told Carmen to secretly get at me, so I wanted to come *clean.*

"Fucking bitch," he mumbled. "Man, I tell you some of these hoes out here ain't shit. What in the hell did she expect you to say? Did she think that you would say fuck me and go work for her slick ass?"

"Yeah, she did. And she offered me more money. Double what you're paying me, and then some."

Mango shook his head. "This a dirty-ass world. And all that whore was gon' double up on was that used-up pussy of hers. She thinks her money can buy her whatever she wants, but I'm here to tell you that money can't buy you everything. I'm glad you let me know what she's been up to. There's a reason I always watched my back with her, and if you think I'm bad, trust me when I say that working for her ass won't be no picnic. She'll stab you in the back in a minute. Catch you off guard and you'll never see the bitch coming. I'm just warning you, just in case a small part of you is giving this shit some consideration. I know the money is tempting, but if and whenever you want more, all you have to do is speak up. Just don't ask now because that bitch Pebbles got me in a rut. When I find her ass, I'ma call you. And trust me when I say I'ma find her soon."

I hoped not, but I didn't say it. And by now, I hoped that Pebbles was long gone.

Later that day, I was at home when I got an interesting text message from Alexis. She'd been calling me for a few days, but I'd been so caught up with what had been going on that I ignored her. Her text message said: I need to come clean. Call me.

I didn't know what that was all about, but when I called her cell phone, she didn't answer. I chilled with my shirt off and sat back on my bed to watch TV. As my eyelids started to flutter, I heard a soft knock at my door. I got off the bed, removed my gun from the nightstand, and made my way to the door. I looked through the peephole, saw that it was Alexis. I wondered how she'd known where I lived, and when I opened the door, I questioned her.

"Bones, I followed you here one night after you left my house. I was just curious about where you lived and who you were living with. Can I come in?"

I really didn't feel like being bothered, but I let her inside. She took off her coat, and underneath it she wore a pair of thigh-high boots and a multicolored minidress. Her hair was full of long curls, and the makeup she had on made her skin look smooth and caramel, instead of pale.

"I got your message earlier, but I figured it would be best for me to come by so that we could holla."

"About what?" I walked to the fridge, then opened it. Grabbed a container of orange juice and started to drink it. Alexis sat at the table. She crossed her legs and started to fidget.

"For starters, I know, or at least I think I know, what happened at Red's place the day Nate shot himself. That he did, but Red was killed by you, not him. I also know that you killed Theo because Brianna told me that you left her in the car, and minutes later, she heard a gunshot. She said that when you returned to the car, blood was on your hands and that you stopped at a gas station to wash them."

Alexis waited for me to respond, but I didn't. I shrugged, then drank more orange juice from the container. She continued.

"I said all of that to say that your secrets are safe with me. No one will ever know what really happened, but I do need some serious cash in order for me to keep my mouth completely shut. The cops keep coming around asking me questions, and Nichelle has been harassing me about spilling the beans and telling her what I know. But I haven't said anything yet. She suspects something, and the last time I spoke to her, she said that she was determined to talk to the police about the last time you saw Theo. See, that little suicide thing didn't work for her. She knows for a fact that Theo wouldn't have ever done anything like that, and when you didn't show up at his funeral, it kind of rubbed her the wrong way."

I released a deep sigh while staring at Alexis. "Anything else?"

"As a matter of fact, yes, there is. A couple more things. I need one million dollars. Soon. And another million for back child support. Brianna is, without a doubt, your daughter. The only reason I had that paperwork manipulated to show that she wasn't was because I was going to let you off the hook. I felt as if I had caused you enough pain and suffering. I wanted you to be free from everything that had happened in the past, and I felt horrible for damaging your friendship with Nate and Theo. But when I saw you with that other bitch at the gas station, I realized how stupid I was. You've been using me, Bones. Just like Nate, you used me. But not anymore. I won't let you do it anymore. It's time that I got something in return from niggas who don't give a fuck about me."

I pulled back a chair, then straddled it backward. While cocking my neck from side to side, I held my stare at Alexis. "I'll ask again. Is there anything else you would like to say?"

"No," she said, rolling her eyes. "I'm done."

"Good. Because I need to hit you with a wake-up call. If I thought for one minute that Brianna wasn't my daughter, you would've been dead. I would've killed you years ago, but I spared your shitty life because I didn't want my child being raised without her mother. And even though yo' ass has been a lousy-ass parent, I know that I ain't done right by her either. I can't give her the kind of life that she deserves to have right now. One day I will be able to, and when that day comes—trust me, it's coming soon—you better have your shit together. If not, I will cut yo' ass up in a thousand and one pieces and feed you to the dogs. Money ain't what you need. What you need is some goddamn brains and parenting classes. You need to get your priorities together and put my fucking daughter above all. Now you got two muthafucking minutes to get the hell out of my face with this bullshit about money and exit. Go rethink some shit and get at me when you're ready to put your big-girl panties on and leave the thongs for hoes who don't have kids and who know how to concoct a better plan. I'm not moved by your threats, and your assumptions about who I done killed are fucking laughable."

Alexis clapped her hands and sat with a fake smile on her face. "This *is* laughable, and how dare you talk about my parenting skills. If you've known all along that Brianna was your daughter, you must ask yourself what exactly have you done for her. I can tell you what I've done . . ."

As Alexis continued to go on and on, I kept my eyes glued to the clock. She was fifteen seconds away from getting the shit knocked out of her. Ten . . . five . . . four, three, two . . . When the minute hand touched the twelve, I tightened my fist and punched her clean in her mouth to silence her. It pained me to do that shit to her, but it had to be this way sometimes, especially when a bitch tried to play me like she did. She hit the floor—hard. I didn't give a fuck about no tears, I ignored the loud cries, and I tuned out her pleas for me to let her go as I dragged her across the floor and to the door. She kicked and screamed, but I threatened to punch her ass again. I opened the door and tossed her ass outside. With a heaving chest and thick wrinkles lining my forehead, I pointed my finger at her.

"Don't *ever* come back here again unless I invite you. And if you knock on this door after I shut it, you *will* regret it."

I slammed the door, then headed back to my room. After lighting a joint, I wiped sweat from my forehead and got back to the movie I had been watching. This time, there were no more interruptions.

The next morning, I got up early, showered, and put on my sweat suit to go for a jog. But just as I touched the doorknob, my cell phone rang. I looked to see who it was. Mango. I quickly answered, but his words on the other end made me stagger.

"I got that bitch," he said. "Get over here as soon as you can."

I wanted to be sure he was talking about Pebbles. "Who? Pebbles?" I said. "If her, where did you find her?"

"She was hiding out at her cousin Sabrina's crib. She let somebody know that Pebbles was there. Now hurry up over here so you can help me deal with this unfortunate situation."

Mango hung up. I was mad as hell at Pebbles for going to LA. Why in the fuck didn't she listen to me? Since she hadn't, her ass was on her own. I wasn't sure what Mango was going to do with her, and why did he need me to help him with this? I kind of had an idea about what he wanted me to do, but I didn't have the guts to do it. And since I didn't, I suspected that shit was on the brink of turning real ugly.

Mango hadn't replaced the car Pebbles had taken to LA yet, so I drove around in a rental. Within forty-five minutes, I was at his place. This time he seemed upbeat. He asked me to follow him to the basement where a lot of dirty work had been done. The second he opened a

heavy steel door with several locks on it, I could see that
Pebbles had found herself in the same predicament as
those white girls. She was bound, but not gagged. Instead
of sitting, she was standing naked. Her hands were tied
above her head, and nothing but filth surrounded her.
Her hair was a tangled mess, and the numerous bald
spots I saw let me know someone had yanked it. Dried
blood was caked underneath her nose, and her eyes
were bruised. As her thin body quivered all over, I took
a hard swallow. It pained me to see her like this. I could
barely look at her—Mango had done quite a number on
her. Then again, he didn't have the guts to do all of this.
Somebody else had to be involved.

Her eyes fluttered as she looked at me. Much sadness
was trapped inside of them. She didn't say one word until
Mango walked over to a corner and came back with a
long wooden stick and a leather whip.

"Pleeease, Mango," Pebbles cried out. "Don't do this. I
am so sorry for everything. I will do whatever I have left
in my power to make things right with you and Big L."

Mango winced, then pulled the stick back. He swung
it like a bat, cracking it across her bare back. As she
screamed out, my heart sank to my stomach.

"You ain't got no power left," he shouted. "And I don't
need you to make shit right for me, especially when I
can do it myself. I haven't had my turn with you yet, and
I wanted Bones to see how I get down on bitches who
betray me."

"I . . . I didn't betray you," Pebbled shouted. "I would
never do that, and you know it. Why won't you listen to
meeeeee?"

Mango responded with several more strikes from the
stick, this time across her ass. Welt marks appeared, and
the stick broke in two from him hitting her so hard.

"Ahhhhhhhh," she hollered. Spit oozed from her mouth, and her weak body was limp.

Mango tossed the half stick, then squeezed the handle to the whip. With gritted teeth, he pulled back, then whipped across her upper body, causing her flesh to slice open and bleed. At that point, every ounce of breath was sucked out of me. Pebbles released an eardrum-busting scream that let us both know she was in severe pain. This had definitely taken me back to the ill treatment my mother received at the hands of her lover. I even thought about what my ancestors had been through when the white man pulled this kind of shit. I couldn't get with a black man like Mango taking things to this level. It left a badass taste in my mouth.

He licked across his crusty lips, displaying a smile as he swung out to whip her again. Pebbles's head was slumped to the side as she looked at me.

"He . . . Help me, Bones," she said in a whisper. "Please don't stand there and let him do this to me."

For the first time in a long time, I felt pain for another. I was hurt, disappointed and pissed at the same time. I blinked to clear the water filling my eyes, and when Mango lifted the whip again, I grabbed his hand.

"That's enough," I said. "You ain't got to do all of that to her."

He snatched the whip away from me, then shot me a devilish gaze that warned me to shut the fuck up.

"*I'll* decide when she's had enough, nigga! This bitch deserves everything she got. She's why I brought you into the fold, and this day was bound to come because she started playing by her rules, not mine. She thought I needed her because she knows how to speak foreign languages and that pussy knows how to make muthafuckas sing. But all hoes can be replaced, and they need to be reminded who the *real* boss is. As soon as I'm done, I

want you to break her muthafucking neck and go dig this
bitch a grave. If you got a problem with that, you need to
speak now or forever hold your peace."

I didn't respond, but the look on my face said it all. I
didn't want to be here. I couldn't bear to see this shit go
down, and there wasn't a chance in the devil's lonely hell
that I would follow through with his order. Not this time.
Not when it came to Pebbles. I didn't say it, but since
there was no movement from me, he damn sure knew it.

Mango sucked his teeth while moving his head from
side to side. "I'll be damned. You done fucked this bitch,
haven't you? She got yo' mind twisted, and that pussy is
wrapped around yo' finger, ain't it?"

"No," I rushed to say. "Ain't nothing like that happened
between us—I just don't like what you doing to her. Yeah,
she fucked up, but everybody is allowed to make some
mistakes. What in the hell you gon' do to me when I'm
out there one day and shit don't go according to your
plans? Are you gon' do *me* the same way?"

Mango didn't hesitate to answer. "You damn right I
will, because nobody . . ." He raised his voice. "I mean,
nobody fucks me over and betrays me! Now stop showing
yo' weakness and get rid of this trick. If you don't break
her neck, I'ma keep beating her ass until every ounce
of flesh is removed from her bones and she bleeds to
death. It's up to you to put her out of her misery before
showtime."

Mango snapped his finger and waited for me to make
the next move. My feet felt as if they were buried in
cement. I couldn't move. Pebbles's whimpering got
louder, and when Mango struck her with the whip again,
that's when I stepped forward. I stood in front of Pebbles,
gazing into her beautiful doe eyes.

"Do it, Bones," she whispered. "End this. They done
beat me, raped me, and now this. I . . . I can't take no
more. I want to die. I *deserve* to die."

I swallowed the huge lump in my throat. I still couldn't honor her or Mango's wishes. And as I stood there in thought, Mango called out to me.

"Do it, you punk-ass muthafucka! Kill that bitch or else I will kill you!"

Before I could respond, he struck me across my arm with the whip. My skin burned—felt as if someone had poured acid on an opened wound. I quickly turned to him displaying a frown. Sweat beads dotted my forehead—my breathing intensified. I had no time for words. This was done, over for Mango . . . his life was a wrap. I pulled my Glock from my sweats and aimed it right at his chest. His eyes shifted from the gun to me.

"If you point that muthafucka at me," he said, "you damn sure better use it."

I cocked my neck to the side, then fired a single shot into his chest, causing him to stagger backward and fall against the concrete wall. His hand trembled over the wound to his chest, and blood seeped from his mouth. Unable to speak, his eyes spoke for him. They confirmed that I too was a dead man. He slowly nodded, and after his eyes shut, his body slumped to the side, hitting the floor.

I could hear Pebbles in the background crying her heart out. In a slight trance, I swung around, then rushed up to untie her. As soon as one of her hands was free, she grabbed my neck and hugged me tight.

"Thank you," she said. "Oh my God, Bones, thank you soooo much."

I untied her other hand, and when she was freed, her body was so weak, bruised, and battered that she couldn't walk. She damn near melted in my arms as I scooped her up to carry her. I was in a rush to get the fuck out of there. I wasn't sure if we would make it out alive or not, but thankfully, we did. Less than an hour later, we were at my loft. Pebbles was in the bathroom chilling in the tub. I stood by the huge picture window, looking out at the city of Chicago and thinking real hard about my next move. Staying here wouldn't work. And by the end of the day, it was likely that Pebbles and I would be history. The only option I had was Carmen. Hopefully, her offer was still on the table, and she wouldn't take issue with what I'd done to Mango. Yeah, I'd have to watch my back with her and settle my beef with some of the others, but it was up to me to calm the noise that would swing my way. I truly believed that some doors would shut because of Mango, but many would open and put me in position to become the next real nigga in charge.